Praise for the book

Invoking familiar place names and provincial icons like the *Bluenose*, Pottie spins a hilarious yarn like a seasoned storyteller.
Vernon Oickle, author of the 'Crows' series

A glorious blend of historical fiction, absurdist comedy, and full-throttle maritime mayhem. Pottie weaves together a caper so riotous and fast-paced that I found myself laughing out loud at least once per page. The tone is sharp, the dialogue crackles and the storytelling somehow straddles multiple time periods while feeling hilariously contemporary. If you love books that mix high-stakes adventure with low-stakes decision-making by teenagers, if you enjoy stories where small-town legends get out of hand, or if you simply need a reason to believe in the sheer power of fiddle-driven anarchy—*The Great Lunenburglary* is the book is for you.
– Jeff Biederman, Award-winning writer for *Life with Derek, Spun Out* and *Radio Free Roscoe*

Not particularly accurate about 1920s radio, but totally accurate about Lockeport, NS (boooo!).
- Prof. Kenn Scott, author of *On Our Wavelength: broadcasting history from a Canadian perspective*

This winning Maritime caper is enough to make a Vancouver boy like me think maybe I've spent a lifetime on the wrong coast. Like good taffy, this one's bright, colourful, full of salt water and guaranteed to stick with you.
- Charlie Demers, CBC's *The Debaters*; author of *Property Values*

This book is a love letter to best friendships and the teenage need to be in a band. It's sweet, heartfelt, and every bit as funny as I would expect from Bryn Pottie.
- Clare Belford, writer, *This Hour Has 22 Minutes*

The Great Lunenburglary
© 2025 Bryn Pottie

Cover and illustration by Sean Skerry • classicgraphic.co
Editor: Andrew Wetmore

ISBN: 978-1-998149-73-5
First edition May, 2025

Moose House Publications
2475 Perotte Road
Annapolis County, NS B0S 1A0
moosehousepress.com
info@moosehousepress.com

Moose House Publications recognizes the support of the Province of Nova Scotia. We are pleased to work in partnership with the Department of Communities, Culture and Heritage to develop and promote our cultural resources for all Nova Scotians.

We live and work in Mi'kma'ki, the ancestral and unceded territory of the Mi'kmaw people. This territory is covered by the "Treaties of Peace and Friendship" which Mi'kmaw and Wolastoqiyik (Maliseet) people first signed with the British Crown in 1725. The treaties did not deal with surrender of lands and resources but in fact recognized Mi'kmaq and Wolastoqiyik (Maliseet) title and established the rules for what was to be an ongoing relationship between nations. We are all Treaty people.

For Nanny.

You were so selfless, I know that being mentioned in this book
would have made you deeply uncomfortable,
especially right on page one.
But writing it helped me cope after you died, so…too bad!

The Great Lunenburglary

The Great Lunenburglary

Prologue

Ten minutes off Highway 103 and right on the Atlantic Ocean, Lunenburg is the most picturesque town on Nova Scotia's South Shore. Much more so than Lockeport, certainly.

A town that loves pretty things and hates change, Lunenburg has preserved its original architecture so well that in 1995 UNESCO recognized it as a world heritage site. Since then, families from all over the world have made Lunenburg (not Lockeport) their destination to putter around and gawk at old boats.

These days, selling debris that washes up on shore to tourists and calling it "sea treasure" is the best way to make a buck in Lunenburg. But for many years, the town's main industry was shipbuilding. In the golden age of sail, Lunenburg shipyards cranked out thousands of vessels.

The most famous of all, or the only one that's remotely famous, really, was the *Bluenose*: the fastest racing schooner ever built.

Plenty of "accurate" books about the *Bluenose* are available at bookstores and gift shops across Nova Scotia. They may have "bibliographies" and "proof they actually happened", but they all miss a deeper truth. In places like Lunenburg, the best stories aren't annotated in museum archives. They're passed down orally from generation to generation, from mosh pit to skate park.

One such legend tells of a ragtag team of townie teens who stole the *Bluenose* for a joyride and wound up saving all of Nova Scotia in the process. It's a story told by Lunenburgers from all walks of life, from the old men who hang around the Tim Horton's all morning to the young misfits who hang around the Tim Horton's all night.

Other than the testimony of fellas who heard from buddies, no historical record exists of these events. The scant few documents that corroborate the story have been inserted throughout this narrative, including these *Lunenburg Herald* articles from three days before our story begins.

BLUENOSE DEFEATS FORD!

October 25, 1922

GLOUCESTER, MA - Life's never ending drudgery became a little less overwhelming for the people of Lunenburg today. Locally built schooner "Bluenose" has once again won the International Fisherman's Cup Race in Gloucester, Massachusetts.

Led by Lunenburg's own Captain Angus J Walters, The Bluenose has defended her title of fastest ship in the world by beating one other boat, the American vessel Henry S Ford.

Because Americans have been beaten at something, no matter how niche, this victory has been embraced as a symbol of national pride across Canada.

"We friggin' did it again, boys! I'm going to get right slammer jammered the moment I get on land," said newly-minted Canadian hero Captain Angus Walters.

When asked about his son, Family Man Captain Walters told reporters, "[I] sure [am very excited to see Angus Junior] at some point."

The Bluenose is scheduled to make her triumphant return to Lunenburg in three days' time, when she and her crew will be greeted by dignitaries, fans, and a special live broadcast of the popular radio programme, "Wharton's Menstrual Powder Presents: Rita MacMurphy's Down Home Kitchen Party."

DEATH OF WEIRD MORON NEARLY RUINS VOYAGE

October 25, 1922

LUNENBURG, NS - Fishing vessel Theresa E Creamer returned from a four month voyage today, reporting an embarrassing casualty at sea that irritated the crew so much, they voted not to lower the flag to half mast.

During a night watch, seaman Jiminy Oickle reportedly abandoned his post, removed all his clothing and jumped into the sea. While no clear motive has been established, many believe he just was trying to get attention. Reports indicate he was the kind of guy who would do something like that.

Oickle's mysterious disappearance nearly caused the vessel to run aground on a reef.

After heroically righting the ship and saving the salt cod aboard, the crew did not deem recovering the body a priority.

He is survived by his wife, Ethel, who released this statement: "Jiminy and I were married off to each other to settle an inter-family dispute over a team of oxen, not by any choice of mine. I deeply apologize for any inconvenience he may have caused in his life or death."

He is also survived by his son Elias, who will be performing with his musical group "Jigtallica" behind Lionel Hynick's shed out in Blue Rocks on October 27th. Their set will be dedicated to Jiminy's memory. Pay what you can.

1: A couple of real Pipperoos

Our story begins the way all great Lunenburg capers do—with a couple of teenagers smoking cigarettes on a bench.

In the 20th century, loitering and tobacco were central to adolescent bonding. To teens in those days, smoking in public was about more than getting a nicotine fix, it was about making a statement. It said to everyone who walked by the Mini Mart, the mall entrance, or whatever the stoop *du jour:* "I'm up to no good! I don't care about my health or my future! I only care about smoking with the people I hang out with. And they only care about me."

This romance is lost on today's teens who just vape over Zoom.

One autumn morning in 1922, fifteen-year-old Elias Oickle rolled his first cigarette of the day. Angus Walters Junior sat on the other end of the bench and watched him roll with the finger dexterity of an expert fiddler.

Every generation of Lunenburgers has one guy who thinks they're too talented for this town, and to this day not one of them has been proven right. In the early 1920s, it was Elias W Oickle. He was a tall and skinny fifteen-year-old, with perfectly slicked-back hair and a straw boater hat, which was not a bad look back then. It was a different time.

Elias had always been "a bit much", which in rural Nova Scotia is the worst thing you can be. But lately his ego had been growing out of control. Months ago, he and Angus Junior had founded their band Jigtallica, and created an aggressive new musical genre—

thrash fiddle. All that unbridled creative freedom had gone to his head.

Until three days ago, when his father's death had brought him back down to earth. Back then, your dad dying at sea was like getting chickenpox: it happened to pretty much everybody, and it was better to get it out of the way early and move on.

But for Elias, the pox left scars.

The ship's actuary had deemed Jiminy's death 'too off-putting', so his pay was withheld and his life insurance was voided. Elias' mother made it clear to her only son that there would be another suspicious death in the family if he didn't go to sea and start earning some money right away.

Two months at sea would really interfere with Jigtallica's momentum, so to make up for lost time, Jigtallica would have to start aggressively touring as soon as Elias got back. Musically, Elias knew they were ready. But Angus Junior would need a little push out of his comfort zone.

Usually, these hangouts at the bench would last for hours on end. Elias would detail his dreams for Jigtallica's future, and the two would brainstorm lyrics for songs about how society is bad. But today, it would have to be cut short. It was already 5:30 AM, which was sleeping in by the standards of 1920s Lunenburg.

The *Theresa E Creamer* sailed at six bells and Elias had to go off with her. Before he finished hacking this dart, Elias had to convince Angus Junior to go on tour with him.

"Ang-Ju, buddy, what are you sayin' today?" Elias asked.

"Uhh, not saying too much today," Angus Junior lied. "Stopping by my dad's *Bluenose* thing, maybe, and then school."

Bluenose captain Angus Walters Senior was the most popular man in Lunenburg, but his son was a chubby little guy with weird hair and no confidence. Less than a year ago, no one had ever invited him to push a hoop with a stick, let alone hang out on a bench. But since he started playing music with Elias, Angus Junior had started coming into his own.

"Uh, great show last night, by the way," he continued. "I mean, not great that the show was because your dad's dead but, uh, you get what I mean."

"Totally! Your tin fluting was so tight. We made my dad's funeral into one of our best sets," Elias said. "We're really finding our voice. Ian Joudrey was there from Lockeport. He didn't even know my dad was dead. He came all the way out just to see us play!"

"Why do you know people from Lockeport?" Angus Junior knew Elias was a rebel, but he didn't know he'd go so far as to trust someone from a different town.

"Give me some credit here! I'm not saying that I like the town of Lockeport or anyone from there. Joudrey's not a bad guy to know, that's all. He books shows all over Shelburne County. Not just Lockeport, but also Barrington Passage, Shag Harbour, Eel River..."

Usually a Jigtallica debrief would have Angus Junior's undivided attention, but today he struggled to listen to this long list of towns. Elias' imminent departure presented a crisis for Angus Junior as well. Without Jigtallica to connect him to the Lunenburg County music scene, he'd go back to being "The Captain's quiet son".

Angus Junior's only hope to stay socially adjusted while Elias was away was for him to become a Real Pipperoo in his own right. That's what cool guys were called back then. Again, it was a different time.

He had a plan:

Step one, bum his first cigarette.
Step two, look cool while smoking it in front of his crush.
Step three, wow everyone with his radio interview.
Step four, use all that impressive stuff to land his first kiss!
Stretch goal, get his dad's attention maybe.

"Think I could skeeze one of those smokes?" he asked, just as he'd rehearsed. "I'm ready to be a Pipperoo."

"Sure thing, Ang-Ju," Elias said, handing him his freshly-rolled cigarette, "Happy to help you out. You're my co-worker in the band, after all. Co-workers help each other, right?"

Had he lived in a time and place where such feelings had names, Elias would have called Angus Junior his best friend.

"I was thinking, co-worker, just because I gotta go off to sea this morning doesn't mean Jigtallica has to end," Elias continued. "If we stick with it, I think we're good enough to play in Halifax one day. You feel it, too, don't you, Ang-Ju? Once we get some time on the road under our belts, we could even be on the radio!"

"The radio? I don't know anything about the radio!" Angus Junior stammered, fumbling with a pack of matches.

For the first time, Angus Junior was keeping a secret from Elias and the guilt was making him extra jumpy. Days ago, he had been approached for an interview by the producers of Nova Scotia's most popular radio show, Wharton's Menstrual Powder Presents: Rita MacMurphy's Down Home Kitchen Party. Miss MacMurphy's people were very clear that the only topics he would be allowed to speak about were his father and the *Bluenose*.

No good could come of telling Elias about this. If he found out, he was sure to come up with some kind of crazy scheme to hijack the show, and Angus Junior would be dragged along as always. The whole town would be there, including Angus Senior. It just wasn't worth the risk.

Elias put an end to Angus Junior's nervous fumbling with the matches by taking the cigarette back and lighting it himself. "I've been in a lot of bands, Ang-Ju," he said. "Tommy Diddler and His Diddlin' Fiddlers, The Irish Singing Boat Boys, The Hard Knock Fifers. But until you and me, until Jigtallica, it never really clicked."

He took a long drag, then handed the cigarette back to Angus Junior. He held up a corked bottle he'd been wearing on a string around his neck. Inside were dozens of rolled up wads of paper.

"Until Jigtallica, I never got to perform any of this stuff," he said, dangling the bottle in front of Angus Junior, "Look at it, Ang-Ju. All the lyrics, fiddle tabs and tin whistle charts we ever wrote. I was going to take them to sea with me, but...I want you to have them while I'm gone."

Elias handed Angus Junior the bottle. "By exchanging this bottle with our lyrics in it, that means we copyrighted them," he said, "We're a legal partnership now."

Even though none of what he said made sense, it was still a nice moment between them. "As such, I have a motion I'd like to bring to a vote," Elias continued.

Angus Junior was far more focused on the cigarette in his left hand than the bottle in his right. He'd been hanging around with smokers for a while now, but had yet to take the plunge himself. If he really went through with this puff, he would forever cross the line between polite young man and lousy, no-good punk.

But smoking was what Pipperoos did, so he went for it and inhaled. The cool smoke hit his nerd lungs and caused an immediate, violent reaction in Angus Junior. He gave a full-body, convulsive cough, spitting out the cigarette and flinging Elias' bottle onto the ground. It rolled down the hill, banked off the sidewalk, and skidded across the street toward the waterfront.

"My songs!" Elias shrieked.

He ran down the hill after the bottle. Elias had not only failed to secure a concrete future for Jigtallica, now he'd endangered all their hard work.

Angus Junior fell off the bench and lay on the ground, coughing and rolling around in the wet morning dew. He was not yet a real Pipperoo.

Neither of them were.

2: Elias annoys someone bigger than him

Lunenburg is built on the side of a steep hill that slopes into the harbour. It's as if the town itself is pushing you into the water.

The Jigtallica bottle was rolling fast down the street with Elias scrambling after it. He could faintly make out the lyrics to *Sea And Destroy* rolling around and around. It was the first song he and Angus Junior ever wrote together.

Back then, Elias had been Tommy Diddler's second fiddler. They were a technically-proficient bar band, but Elias quickly grew tired of playing the same old traditional songs about bogs and the logs therein.

One night, Captain Angus Walters hired them for a kitchen party to celebrate the launch of his new schooner, the *Bluenose*. At the last minute, the band's tin flutist bailed on the gig after coming down with consumption, so Tommy asked if there was a tin flute player in the crowd. Angus Walters Junior timidly walked up on stage, hoping maybe his dad would notice him if he joined the band and saved the party.

Sadly, then as now, blowing into a recorder-like instrument in the kitchen is not a positive way to get a parent's attention. Angus Senior ignored it, but Elias didn't.

Music was something that Elias actually had to work at; it never came easy to him. Angus Junior, on the other hand, was a total natural, and Elias could tell right away. This was the kind of talent he had to surround himself with if he wanted to get to the next level.

After the party, Elias and Angus Junior stayed up the whole night jamming and writing together. The riffs Angus Junior came up with were like nothing Elias had ever imagined. But Elias took all those raw ideas and shaped them into a tight eight and a half minute song.

Tommy hated it, but that didn't matter. Elias had learned all he could as a Diddlin' Fiddler. He talked his way out of his contract, formed Jigtallica with Angus Junior and never looked back. From then on, Elias was more than a gig musician; he was an obnoxious teenage artist.

Elias and Angus Junior spent the next 18 months writing aggressive songs like *Master Of Poop Decks*, *Sea Shells But Who's Buyin?* and *St. Anchor*. Their resounding win at the Feltzen South Battle Of The Bands was a statement to the South Shore music scene. They followed that up with strong performances at kitchen parties from Stonehurst to Pinehurst.

This was the happiest time of Elias' life. He'd never had a friend like Angus Junior before, someone who liked being creative instead of just drinking behind buildings and smoking in front of other buildings.

Angus Junior had never had a friend before, period.

Three nights ago Jigtallica got a standing ovation at Topsl's Tavern in Bridgewater. Any musician worth their salt will tell you, Bridgewater crowds are the toughest in Lunenburg County.

As he walked offstage, Elias' happiness hit its high water mark. He'd worked hard, made the right connections and now it was all coming together.

But that night, out in the Atlantic, his stupid dad's stupid death brought it all to a halt.

~

All that hard work was scrunched up in a bottle now rolling out of control toward the ocean. It hit the bottom of the hill and skidded onto a busy wharf. Dozens of fishermen and sailors hustled along the waterfront, paying no attention to the bottle rolling around the dock.

Elias scrambled after it, pushing his way through the crowd. "Look out!" he yelled, "Stop kicking that bottle around, guys! There's lyrics in there! And tabs!"

Elias' calls for help fell on deaf ears. If some big-time Halifax songwriter's lyrics were getting knocked around, everyone would've stopped what they were doing and helped. These ignorant wharf rats just didn't support local creators.

In his haste, Elias accidentally bumped into Polluto, a big, gruff fisherman with a reputation around town for hating getting bumped into.

"Watch where yer going, landlubber!" Polluto yelled.

"So what if I lub the land? Land rules!" Elias said.

Polluto grabbed Elias by the shirt and held him up. "You're Jiminy's boy, ain't ye?"

"Let go of me!" Elias yelled, "I've gotta get my bottle!"

"It ain't even six in the morning! Get some help, young fella!"

"I don't need help! I need you to let go of me!" Elias struggled to free himself, "That bottle is gonna win me an East Coast Music Award someday! Now let me go!"

"Just like yer old man!" Polluto scoffed. "Bumping all around and speaking nonsense at people! Ye think yer better than me cause yer in a band? Y'ain't!"

Elias scanned the wharf for the bottle, but it was lost in the morning shuffle. He had to get away and search for it. "I don't think I'm better than you, and I'm really sorry that I bumped you like that," he said, lying about both things, "but I'm sure we both have decks to swab and places to be. Let's just move on with our lives."

Polluto slapped Elias' boater hat off his head and into the water. "I don't take orders from teenagers!" he yelled, "except the first mate, I guess. But he's nineteen, that's different!"

The reminder of his own career setbacks coupled with Elias' cocky attitude triggered a rage in Polluto, and he shoved him to the ground.

Lying flat on his back, Elias looked to his left and saw that he was now eye to eye with the Jigtallica bottle. At the edge of the wharf, it leaned precariously against a cleat. It was safe for the moment, but it would only take a slight breeze to knock it into the water.

Elias started to crawl toward it, but Polluto stood over him.

"Wait!" Elias protested, "Haven't you heard the new superstition? Beating up a kid on the dawn of a voyage brings rough seas!"

Polluto had never heard this, but he had a hard time keeping up with which superstitions were accurate and which were just old wives' tales. He was already running late, so he didn't have time to verify it with any of the passing fishermen.

"Ah, y'ain't worth it!" he muttered, and stormed off.

Elias immediately bolted for the edge of the wharf and nabbed the bottle before it tumbled into the deep. He lay on his back, caught his breath, and closely inspected his genius scraps of paper, making sure they were all still there. The threat of losing important lyrics like those to *Holy Wharf... The Punishment Due* had subsided, but the struggle was far from over.

No matter what, Elias knew that his future in an artist-hating town like Lunenburg would just be one confrontation after another. He only had fifteen minutes before the *Theresa E Creamer* set sail, but he got up and went to find Angus Junior. He wasn't leaving town without a firm yes on the Jigtallica tour.

3: Gwendolyn Risser and the deadly wager

The Bluenose's Fisherman's Cup victory had a profound effect on the psyche of Lunenburg's citizenry. Captain Angus Walters had shown everyone that it was possible to do more with your life than kill as many sea creatures as possible until your body falls apart. Nova Scotia's most frowned upon sins, confidence and pride, were beginning to blossom in Lunenburg.

On the morning of the *Bluenose*'s homecoming, a buzzing crowd of grizzled fishermen gathered at the waterfront to watch her triumphant return. No North American audience would be so giddy with anticipation again until the Beatles performed on *The Ed Sullivan Show*.

Nearby, Angus Walters Junior lay in the wet grass, recovering from his brush with coolness.

"Good morning Angus Junior," Gwendolyn Risser said, approaching him. "The probabilities were good that I'd see you today, but I did not predict that I'd find you laying down."

Angus Junior quickly scrambled to his feet. No matter what culture or era, no teen has ever wanted to look weird in front of their crush.

Gwen was a bookish girl with a deep love for statistics and probabilities. If she'd grown up in the 1980s, she would've built a computer in her garage. In the 2000s, she'd have been an online poker champion. But as a product of 1920s Lunenburg, the only practical application of data analysis that Gwen could think of was plotting courses for sailing ships. As far back as she could remember, she always wanted to be a navigator.

"Uh, hi, Gwen. I smoke now!" said Angus Junior, theatrically waving the cigarette around, "It's just something I picked up from my music friends."

He almost took another drag, but instead threw it on the ground and stomped it out. "This one's pretty much done," he said.

"I'm not sure smoking suits you." Gwen told him. She was disappointed to see another example of Elias' creeping influence.

To a navigator, the best course is the safest and most predictable one. Before Angus Junior had joined Jigtallica, he was the dullest and most predictable guy in town. Gwen found that deeply attractive.

"So...The *Bluenose* is coming in today. Not that I care or anything." Angus Junior pivoted. "But I'm supposed to talk about it on this thing called the radio, I'm not sure if you've heard of it. Of course you have, sorry. Anyway, it doesn't have to be a big thing, but I was wondering if maybe—"

"Hey there, Ang-Ju!" Elias interrupted as he arrived. "Can you believe this crowd? They'll be lining up like this to see Jigtallica some day!"

Elias lit up a cigarette, and Angus Junior felt relieved when he didn't offer him one.

"I think maybe I'd better hold onto the bottle after all," Elias continued. "I'd never forgive you if something happened to it, and I don't want to hate you. Speaking of which, Gwen, what are you sayin'?"

"Oh, good morning, Elias," she said as she scribbled in her notebook. "Your posture is very poor today. I'll add that to my dataset."

"Your what? Actually, who cares? Gwen, can you give us some space?" Elias asked. "I've got a voyage to catch and, before I shove off, Ang-Ju and I need to talk shop."

"Oh, I know about the voyage," Gwen answered, "The girls at the Academy have a wager about whether you'll survive. As the one who knows the most math, I'm in charge of calculating the odds. Hmm…I shouldn't have told you that. It could influence your behaviour and skew the outcome."

"You're betting on my death?" Elias asked. "What is wrong with you?"

"I'm not actually placing a bet, I'm simply calculating the odds of your survival so that others can bet."

"Seriously, Ang-Ju? This is the girl you have a crush on?" Elias asked, incredulous.

"What? I never said I have a crush on Gwen," Angus Junior said. "Uh, unless—"

Gwen put her finger to Angus Junior's lips. "We'll discuss this later. Matters of the heart are notoriously difficult to forecast and I already have too many numbers to crunch," she whispered. "I have to get to the Academy while the blackboard is still free."

"Gwen, wait!" Angus Junior called out as she strode away.

"Let her go, man. Love is a distraction. We have to be focused," Elias said, putting his hand on Angus Junior's shoulder.

"Why do you have to talk about her like that?" Angus Junior asked, brushing the hand away.

"Because she's trying to ruin the band! She's got you writing ballads, for frig's sake!"

"Which you never put on the set list anyway!"

"Because we're thrash fiddle, Ang-Ju! We play hard music! We can't just throw in a sappy, slow number because you want to impress Math Girl. It's not our sound!"

The fact that they were even debating this was just another example of Gwen's creeping influence. She was trying to manipulate Angus Junior into being her boyfriend and it was undoing all the work Elias had done to manipulate him into being his sidekick. There was no telling what would happen when he went to sea and left the two of them alone for months.

Elias took a hard drag on his cigarette. "That said, Ang-Ju, our sound can evolve. We can workshop your songs on the road. I hear they like that kind of stuff out in Shelburne County. It was gonna be a surprise, but I have a tour lined up for us when I get back. The whole South Shore! We're gonna play Mahone Bay, Blandford, Port Mouton, Lockeport—"

The gathering crowd of jittery Lunenburgers was getting too loud for Angus Junior to listen to another town list. It was the last thing he wanted to hear, anyway.

Jigtallica was fun and Elias was a good guy, but his ego was never satisfied. With each new song, the fiddle solos got longer and longer. The schedule was getting punishing. They were sometimes playing gigs in both Chester and Chester Basin on the same night. Now he was going off about Lockeport, of all places. Where would it end? Yarmouth?!

"—Petite Riviere, New Germany, Vogler's Cove—" Elias continued.

"Uh, can we talk about this when you get back?" asked Angus Junior.

"What?" Elias yelled. The crowd was now too big and loud for a conversation to be possible.

"Thar he blows!" yelled a frenzied crowd member, as he scooped up Angus Junior and held him aloft. "The captain's quiet son!"

"I need his hair for me scrapbook!" yelled another *Bluenose*-crazed onlooker.

"So that's a yes on the tour then?" Elias shouted.

"We'll talk about it when you get back!" Angus yelled from a distance.

By now, he was being passed around by well-wishers, in what

many have cited as Lunenburg County's first crowd surf.

"Okay, then!" yelled Elias, "Have a good one!"

But neither of them would have good ones. Elias could scheme and plot all he wanted, but it didn't matter anymore and he knew it. He would be a different person when he got back from sea, and so would Angus Junior. Very few teenage bands can survive a change like that.

Jigtallica wouldn't even survive the next 24 hours.

4: Angus Junior on the air

The following is a transcript of the radio show, "Wharton's Menstrual Powder Presents Rita MacMurphy's Down Home Kitchen Party." This episode was first broadcast on October 28, 1922.

ANGUS JUNIOR
Uh… Whoa. Is that a real microphone? I've never seen one up close. Hello? Hello?

Loud THUMPING and microphone FEEDBACK.

ANNOUNCER
Get away from that! What's wrong with you, kid?
(Clears throat)
Live from fabulous Lunenburg Harbour, it's a very special episode of Rita MacMurphy's Down Home Kitchen Party! Brought to you by Wharton's Menstrual Powder, the powder that I assume you ladies know what to do with. Here to help us bring home the *Bluenose*, let's hear it for your host, the lovely and talented Rita MacMurphy!

Crowd CHEERING.
Cheering continues, then trails off.
Long pause, followed by radio STATIC.

ANNOUNCER
What's that stretching motion you're making, Doug? What? Doing it more emphatically doesn't help me know what it means. Use words.

DOUG
(distant voice)
Stretch for time!

ANNOUNCER
Oh…I get it now. Ugh. Okay, is anybody in the crowd celebrating anything? A birthday maybe? An anniversary?

Radio STATIC.

ANNOUNCER
Anybody here from out of town? Hmm, you all seem to be pointing at that guy. You sir, where are you visiting from?

MAN
Lockeport.

Crowd BOOS.

ANNOUNCER
Lockeport? Isn't that the place with the crazy mayor? Your town stinks so bad, even people from Halifax know about it!

Crowd CHEERS.

MAN
The Mayor actually makes some good points, see? You gotta listen

to what he says and not the newspapers!

Crowd BOOS.

ANNOUNCER
Oh, thank God, she's here. Alright, let's take that Lockeport-hating energy, and turn it into love for your host, Nova Scotia's loveliest lass, Rita MacMurphy!

Crowd CHEERS.

RITA MACMURPHY
Ahoy, darlings! You're so kind.

ANNOUNCER
Out all night again, I see. One of these days I'm gonna…

Muttering fades into distance, car door SLAMS, car DRIVES AWAY.

RITA MACMURPHY
I'm Rita MacMurphy and welcome to my kitchen party! Today we're celebrating The Bluenose, a simply marvellous boat! And I understand we've got the captain's fabulous son here with us. You must be simply bursting with pride for your pop, hey little one?

Sound of NERVOUS BREATHING.

RITA MACMURPHY
Speak up, darling.

ANGUS JUNIOR
Whoa. You really are Rita MacMurphy! You sang on "Lukey's Boat" for Redfish Records in 1918. Ronny Hebb played the tin flute, Pete Mosher on fiddle and Ezra Savory on drums. I love that record.

RITA MACMURPHY
You are fabulously off-putting, darling.

> *Cannon FIRES in the distance.*
> *Crowd CHEERS.*

RITA MACMURPHY
Ladies and gentlemen, that terribly loud cannon signals that the *Bluenose* has been sighted. And there she is, sailing into the harbour! Let's welcome her back, shall we? Nova Scotia style!

> *She SINGS in Gaelic.*
> *CHEERING intensifies.*

RITA MACMURPHY
The *Bluenose* has just fabulously docked. Captain Angus Walters is holding the Fisherman's Cup trophy above his head. Whether the applause is for him or for my singing is not entirely clear. One thing is certain, the crowd is going wild here at Rita MacMurphy's Down Home Kitchen Party.

And you'll go wild at home for Wharton's Menstrual Powder. I don't use it myself, nor do I understand how it should be applied. But I've been assured that it does not cause any medical harm.

Captain Walters, darling, how does it feel to bring the Fisherman's Cup back to Lunenburg?

CAPTAIN ANGUS WALTERS
Makes me feel like getting right hammered and starting a friggin' riot! Am I right, Lunenburg? Fastest schooner in the world, baby!

Frenzied CHEERING.

CAPTAIN ANGUS WALTERS
I love this town too much to smash it up, so let's all take the train to Halifax and tear that place apart!

Crowd SCREAMING.

CAPTAIN ANGUS WALTERS
Wait, Junior, is that you? What are you doing here? Are you skipping school? Don't lie to me, boy! I'm a chill dude, but not a chill dad!

ANGUS JUNIOR
I'm just skipping the morning, I was gonna go after lunch.

CAPTAIN ANGUS WALTERS
For shame! And is that tobacco I smell? Let me sniff you, boy!

Very loud SNIFFING.

CAPTAIN ANGUS WALTERS
I never should've permitted you to spend your time playing little shanties with that squirmy kid. Now you're smoking and shirking your school duties! You march yourself up to that schoolhouse this minute young man, and then come straight back here after to guard the boat, you hear me?

ANGUS JUNIOR
(shaky voice) You know what, Dad?

CAPTAIN ANGUS WALTERS
You got something to say to me, boy?

Angus Junior WHIMPERS.

CAPTAIN ANGUS WALTERS
Well? Spit it out!

ANGUS JUNIOR
Aaargh!

Rapid FOOTSTEPS fade into the distance.

RITA MACMURPHY
And there he goes, ladies and gentlemen! What a dreadfully uncomfortable aside. Now that you've fabulously berated your son, Captain Walters, how about a tour of the *Bluenose* for my listeners?

CAPTAIN ANGUS WALTERS
No time, ma'am. Hey everyone! I hear Halifax has got a new Rub and Tugboat circling the harbour! To the train station, boys!

Crowd CHANTS "Rub and Tugboat! Rub and Tugboat!"

RITA MACMURPHY
A very abrupt and unprofessional exit by Captain Walters, and by most of the men in town. Thank you all for listening, darlings, and until next time, ha cha cha and away we go!

Pause and radio STATIC.

RITA MACMURPHY
We filled the full hour, right? Doug darling, what's that stretching motion you're making? Oh, stretch for time. Alright, well…

Rita SINGS in Gaelic for 37 minutes.
Music FADES OUT.

END OF PROGRAM

5: Schemer versus *Creamer*

After waving goodbye to Angus Junior, Elias shuffled off down the waterfront. Even on a momentous day like the *Bluenose*'s homecoming, there were too many fish in the ocean for Lunenburg's comfort. In five minutes, The *Theresa E Creamer* was casting off to kill a few thousand more, and Elias had no choice but to go with them.

As the last of the supplies were loaded on board, The *Creamer*'s first mate hummed a tune and supervised. Elias grimaced. People at sea only hummed and sang the most clichéd shanties. From a musical standpoint, this voyage would totally lack the kind of experimentation and risk-taking that defined Jigtallica.

"What are you sayin', sea guy?" he said as he approached. "My dad's dead, so my mom told me I'm supposed to come down here and beg for a job on your boat."

"Jiminy's boy, eh? You're not gonna jump overboard on us like he did, are you?"

"And deprive the world of my band? As if!" Elias scoffed.

"Hmm... Alright, get on board," the first mate said. "We need a throater."

Elias walked onto the ship, "Now, was I supposed to bring any clean clothes or soap or anything, or is that stuff provided?"

Moments later, the *Theresa E Creamer* cast off and Elias' first voyage began. On the wharf, women waved goodbye to their husbands, sons and side pieces. Elias didn't look back.

The first mate showed him the ropes. "These ones are for tying knots with, and these ones are just for pulling on," he said. "But as a throater, you won't really need to worry about that. You just focus on slitting fish throats."

"Slitting what?" Elias mumbled. "Sorry, I kind of spaced out for a second there."

Elias was fixated on everyone's hands. Everywhere he looked, someone was getting fish hooks jabbed through their knuckles, their palms burned by rope, or their fingertips pinched by crabs. He could count the people onboard who still had all their fingers on one hand, and he was one of a very select few who could.

"Honestly, I was hoping for a position a little more geared toward the arts, if that's available," he said. "I really need to keep my fingers in fiddling shape. I make my living playing a very technical, speedy kind of music, you see."

"You make your living slitting fish throats. But with a little hard work, in a few years you can move up to chopping their heads off," the first mate said, then looked up at the sun. "I'm late for a meeting below deck. Polluto here will take care of you."

Elias gulped as he turned and saw Polluto, the big fisherman who'd slapped his hat off, towering over him.

"Well, well, well me b'ys. We've got ourselves a future ECMA winner on our hands!" Polluto said with a laugh.

"Yeah boss!" said Petey, his squeaky-voiced little friend. "He's a regular Rita MacMurphy over here, huh? I seen her in town last night. Pretty neat, huh, boss?"

"Actually, Rita MacMurphy is a lot more mainstream than the stuff I play," Elias said. "My sound is less traditional...Wait a minute, you saw her in town?"

"Yeah! She was playing crib all night with some buddies down at the Knot Pub. I heard tell she threw up all over the drapes at the Boscawen," Petey said. "Pretty cool story, huh, boss? We should hang out on land too, not just out here!"

"Shut up the both of ye!" boomed Polluto, grabbing Elias once again. He noticed as Elias instinctively clutched the bottle of Jigtallica lyrics around his neck. "Don't like traditional stuff eh? Well, we got a tradition around here for ye! Keep away!"

Elias struggled as Polluto yanked the bottle off of his neck and threw it to Petey. "Guys, please! My lyrics are in there!" pleaded Elias.

His words fell on deaf ears.

"And my tabs!"

"Thanks for including me in your game, boss!" Petey, said, tossing it back to Polluto. "Keep away!"

"Stop!" Elias shouted. "Or I'll report you to HR!"

"Report us to Haddock Randy? Go right ahead!" Polluto said. "Hey, Ran, we're playin' keep away!"

A burly man named Haddock Randy grabbed the bottle and gave a hearty laugh, then threw it to Cod Randy, who threw it to Haddock Dave, who threw it back to Polluto.

"What's this say?" Polluto asked Petey, pointing to a lyric in the bottle.

"I can teach you how to read if you want, boss. It'll give us something to do together back on land!" offered Petey. "This says, Cod Hates Us All."

"Well, I hates us all standing around doing nothing," Haddock Randy said. "Let's get our minds on our work!"

He threw the bottle over Elias' head, and over the side. The whole crew laughed, happy to see a young person with dreams get taken down a peg.

"Sorry lad, that was a bit too far, but 'twas all in good fun. Gotta give up your land life to fit in at sea. Your old man never learned that lesson, and now he's dead," Polluto said, "Now, to cut a fish's throat ye just gotta remember me ten step process."

Elias nodded and gave a blank stare. All of his available brain-power had been diverted to scheming. The only copy of his life's work had splashed down into the ocean and he couldn't just abandon it there.

Jigtallica had been so close to making it. But now he had no songs, and by the end of this voyage, he'd have fewer fingers. Even if he made it back unscathed, 'Miss Math' Gwendolyn Risser would have had months alone with Angus Junior to chip away at him with her pro-school, anti-band propaganda. He'd never be able to re-build.

"They used to give gloves to new throaters, but I put a stop to it." Polluto continued, waving a knife around. "They just slow ye down!"

Elias looked back at Lunenburg. On the wharf where the *Bluenose* was docked, he saw a crew taking down a portable radio tower. Had Polluto's little friend been telling the truth? Was Rita MacMurphy really in town? If he and Angus Junior could find Rita, they could talk her into listening to them play. The second she heard the opening riff of *Tide The Lightning*, she'd sign Jigtallica to a record deal and put them on the radio.

"They say the window to a fish's soul is in the throat," Polluto mused. "Hey! Are ye paying attention? This here's insightful stuff!"

If Rita MacMurphy had actually gotten drunk enough last night to throw up at the Boscawen Inn, she wouldn't leave without taking advantage of the hotel's continental breakfast. The Wentzell sisters were on shift today, and they were by far the slowest and least-dedicated employees in Lunenburg County. The *Theresa E Creamer* wasn't even out of the harbour. If he really swam for it, Elias could make it to shore, rally Angus Junior, and give Rita MacMurphy the show of her life before the Wentzells even got around to bringing her the bill.

Every second's hesitation just gave Elias more distance to swim.

He had to decide now. Learn a viable skill and gain job experience, or risk everything to interrupt a hungover woman's breakfast?

Elias bolted across the *Creamer*'s deck.

"Where ye going, young fella? The throats are right here!" Polluto shouted.

The *Creamer* crew watched in shock as Elias dove off the side of the boat into the freezing-cold harbour. He surfaced seconds later, gave them a wave and swam toward his bobbing bottle of lyrics.

"Man overboard!" yelled Polluto, and made for a lifeboat.

"Leave him be," the first mate said. "No room for jumpers in our crew. Sorry, Polluto, but it looks like your promotion to head chopper is on hold for this trip."

"Y'arr!" Polluto yelled, which is an empty sailor exclamation nowadays, but it really meant something back then.

He felt betrayed as he watched Elias swim back to Lunenburg. To think, he was going to take him under his wing and make him the new Petey. He could've been the Lunenburg throat GOAT, but now he was just another loser with a dream, like his old man.

"I'll make that boy slit these fish throats if it's the last thing I do!" he shouted. "You ain't seen the last of me, young fella!"

"Me too, boss!" Petey chimed in.

6: The seven times table

Up at the Lunenburg Academy, math class with Schoolmaster Karl Hennigar was underway. According to the educational standards of the time, children learned mathematics by reciting the multiplication tables over and over again and were hit with a cane whenever they made a mistake. As he was a World War I veteran, this life of monotony punctuated by sudden bursts of violence suited Hennigar just fine.

"Seven times five is 35," the students droned.

As he mumbled along, Angus Junior slumped in his chair and mentally licked his wounds. His Pipperoo plans lay in ruin. Instead of getting a kiss, he was reciting the seven times tables with the other kids in town lame enough to show up for school on Bluenose Homecoming Day.

"Seven times six is 42."

His first cigarette was a total bust. Elias had made smoking look so easy. He made everything look easy. Making friends, bantering on stage, believing in himself. Sure, he was "a bit much", but was that really the worst thing?

"Seven times seven is 49."

Elias was the only person in town who didn't care who Angus Junior's dad was. He had shown him a world where people cared more about aggressive music than about fishing boat races. A world where Angus Junior's own talents mattered.

Angus Junior had repaid this kindness by lying to the best friend he ever had, and it had blown up in his face. Radio listeners all over Nova Scotia heard him get in trouble with his dad and then cry about it. Would it really have been worse with Elias there?

"Seven times eight is 57."

SMACK.

"Ow!"

Angus Junior's heart ached more than his freshly-caned knuckles. He looked over at Gwen, who was deep in her calculations. As soon as she heard about how bad he blew it on the radio, the chances of a first kiss would become, as she would say, statistically insignificant.

Maybe it was for the best. Within months of their first kiss, many of his teenage contemporaries were married, with a baby on the way. He wasn't sure if he was ready for that kind of commitment, even with Gwen.

"Seven times nine is 63. 63, I said! Don't hit me, please."

Angus Junior was less sure of himself than ever. His dad was back on land, his best friend was out to sea and his crush was in a world of her own. He needed a sign.

"Seven times 10 is—" Collective gasp!

Dripping wet and covered in seaweed, Elias had kicked open the classroom door. "Ang-Ju, what are you sayin', buddy? Look, I got us a big time showcase at the Boscawen Inn, but we gotta go right now."

Angus Junior had so many questions, like "What are you talking about?" and "What are you doing here?" but could only manage the catchall, "Uh…What?"

"Ang-Ju, you said we'd talk when I got back. Well, I'm back!" Elias said. "So, let's talk! On our way to the Boscawen, preferably."

"It's really not a good time, Elias," Angus Junior said, acutely feeling everyone's eyes on him. "We're just about to start saying the eights."

"Well, I eight to say it, but you're being selfish!" Elias chastised him, "You're a once in a generation tin-fluting talent. But you're sitting here, hiding your gifts from the world, and for what? Basic math? We have a chance at the big time here!"

"Elias Oickle, you drop-out trench rat, evacuate this house of learning at once!" Schoolmaster Hennigar shouted.

Elias scoffed. "I'm 15. I don't have to listen to teachers anymore!"

Everyone went "Oooh!" emboldening Elias.

"Yeah! Plus I heard around town that in the war, you only fought against the Austro-Hungarians. Not even real Germans!" he continued, "And that you used to pee in a rag and smell it."

"That was to survive mustard gas attacks." Hennigar tried to explain to the snickering class. "Everyone did that!"

"He admits it!" Elias crowed. "Ew! Gross!"

Everyone laughed and cheered.

To reassert his dominance over third period math, Hennigar took a Luger out of his desk and pointed it at Elias. It was unclear if school board policy permitted teachers to carry sidearms, but it wasn't a conversation anyone at the board office wanted to have with the Schoolmaster.

"You have ten seconds to retreat with your life!" he yelled "Angus Junior, remain in your seat!"

Elias had faced down the prospect of a career in the trades that day, a fate worse than death. He wasn't about to let a homicidal math teacher stop him now. "Ang-Ju, you don't have to listen to this pee freak!"

"Ten..." Hennigar started counting.

"Angus Junior," Gwen warned. "The risk/reward ratio here is very badly skewed against Elias."

"Nine..."

"Thanks for that, Gwen." said Elias. "But let's let him make up his own mind, shall we?"

"Eight…"

"Uh…" mumbled Angus Junior. He'd never been put on the spot like this before. Someone usually made all his decisions for him.

"Seven…"

"Uhhhhhh…"

"Six…"

"Ang-Ju, if you stay in this classroom, you'll never be more than the son of the *Bluenose* captain. Years from now, who's gonna care about the *Bluenose*? Jigtallica is forever! I believe in that and I believe in you. I may be a good showman, but we both know you're the real musical talent. I can't do it without you!"

"Five…"

"You count at such a weird pace!" Elias shouted at Hennigar.

"Four, three, two—"

"Wait!" yelled Angus Junior, rising from his desk.

He had been following his own instincts all day, and it had gotten him nowhere. Elias believed in him, maybe it was time to believe in Elias. Angus Junior walked toward the exit.

"Mr. Walters Junior," Hennigar threatened. "If you walk out that door, I'll do worse than shoot you. I'll tell your dad."

Angus Junior looked the teacher dead in the eye. "Tell him to smell my pee!"

The class looked at him, not quite getting it.

"Hmm." Elias said, and they quietly left together.

Hennigar put the gun back in his desk drawer, ran his fingers through his hair, and cleared his throat.

"Alright, everyone, excitement's over. Eight times one is eight."

"I get what you were going for with the pee thing, but it didn't quite work," Elias critiqued as he and Angus Junior walked through the Academy halls. "Why would your dad smell your pee? It's the teacher who does that."

As they walked out the front door, Angus Junior began to feel the weight of what he had just done. He had put his future in the hands of a guy who'd just crawled out of the sea and was now picking through a pile of cigarette butts on the ground.

"Mine haven't dried out yet," Elias explained.

"Uh…so. This showcase, when is it exactly?" Angus Junior asked.

"Haven't totally nailed down a time." Elias said, fumbling with a pack of soaking wet matches. "Basically, it's whenever we find Rita MacMurphy's hotel room and lock ourselves in with her until she agrees to listen to us."

Had he known this was the extent of the plan, Angus Junior probably would've stayed in school.

7: Rick's role

Rick Hirtle sat at Elias' kitchen table, smoking a cigarette and drinking a carton of Beep.

No one quite remembered when Rick moved to Lunenburg or where he came from. He came in on the fog one night and, before long, it was like he'd always been there. At the wise old age of 20, Rick was the only man in town who had reached the age of legal majority without getting disfigured or married, making him Lunenburg's hottest bachelor.

Because of conservative social norms on land and high mortality rates at sea, the South Shore had a large community of lonely widows who never remarried. Rick had carved out a niche for himself, providing comfort and companionship in exchange for room and board.

Sometimes for long stays, sometimes just for one night. Your mileage may vary.

Rick wiped a bit of cigarette ash off of his bare chest. His shirt had ripped during that morning's comforting session, and Elias' mother was upstairs mending it.

He could be very happy here, but he knew this gig was temporary. Come what may, his business had to conclude before Elias got back from sea. He had made a vow to himself to never take on another client with a teenage son. Not after what happened last time.

Suddenly, the front door started to jiggle. This was unusual. For devil-tricking purposes, people in Nova Scotia use the side or back door, never the front.

The jiggle grew into a thump, so Rick got up and answered the door. There stood a damp Elias.

"Oh, hey. What are you sayin', Rick?" Elias greeted him. "Can I skeeze one of those smokes by any chance?"

"Elias, me son, I didn't expect ye back so soon," said Rick. "What happened to the tobacco pouch I gave ye?"

"Long story," Elias answered, taking a cigarette. "Wait, what are you doing here? Is that why the back door was locked? Are you...working?"

In the days before people from Ontario started moving to Lunenburg, the doors in town were seldom locked. But years of nosy-neighbour incidents made Rick institute a locked-door policy during work hours.

Rick sighed. "Aye, ye got me dead to rights. I'm working on your ma. Big time."

He felt a bit sleazy about this gig, but he had to take it. He'd been staying with Zelda Knickle after her husband had been kicked in the head by an ox. But he'd woken up from his coma and left Rick in a tight spot.

When he was off duty, Rick was a big supporter of the Lunenburg County music scene. After catching their first set at the Legion hall, Rick became a Jigtallica fan. Last week, he was backstage at Topsl's Tavern, congratulating Elias and Angus Junior on their set when Elias got the news his dad had passed. Rick started making overtures to Elias' mother the following day, and by the night of the funeral, he was move-in ready.

"You know what, Rick? It doesn't matter," Elias said. "I'm just here to grab my fiddle and hit the road."

Rick stepped outside and shut the door. He put his arm around Elias and took him into his confidence. "Me son, of all the kids I ever been like a father to, ye worry me the most. That's why I hate to put you out when you're having a rough go. But you gotta boot 'er outta here, lad. I ain't gonna end up like Ronnie Crouse."

"I don't know who Ronnie Crouse is and I'm sure that what you and my mother have is very special," Elias said. "But I need that fiddle, so get out of my way!"

"Ronnie Crouse used to service widows up in New Minas. Taught me all I know about the business. One night Ronnie comforted The Widow Jenkins so good, it put her right to sleep. While she was out cold, Ronnie threw a little shindig in her back shed. Didn't take long for all the widows and future widows to hear: Ronnie Crouse can't be trusted. After that, not a single lady in the whole valley would feel him up for a hot meal. In my line of work, your word is more important than your dink. Sorry, me son, but I can't go against your Ma's wishes."

Rick stood his ground in front of the door. He wasn't a real step-dad, but he could fight like one. Elias knew he needed to make a deal.

"I don't want to tell you your business, Rick. But living with my mother won't turn out any better for you than it did for me. My dad's life insurance was voided for being a creep and I just jumped off the *Creamer* before getting a dime. Maybe not today, maybe not tomorrow, but someday soon she is going to tell you to get a job. I'm here to offer you one right now—manager of Jigtallica."

"What's it pay?" Rick asked, intrigued.

"Nothing at first," Elias answered, taking a drag from his cigarette, "but there's benefits. Angus Junior and I are on our way to meet Rita MacMurphy, Nova Scotia's most eligible three-time widow. As our manager, you'll be in charge of negotiating our contract with her alone."

"Go way with you, me son!" Rick said, "A rich Halifax widow? I'm good at what I do, but I ain't ready for The Show."

"You said it yourself, Rick. Your word is more important than your dink. Big city dinks must be more or less the same, but no one's word is stronger than yours. Rita's got the whole package. Her first husband's money, her second husband's record label and her third husband's radio connections. With all that out of her system, she must be ready to settle down and marry for love!"

Rick had never seduced a widow from a town bigger than Bridgewater, let alone a Scotia-wide celebrity like Rita MacMurphy. But Rick's situation in Lunenburg was starting to run its course. If he didn't bet on himself now, he might never get another chance.

"Go get your fiddle, me son. I'm in." he said "Your ma's sewing upstairs. You should be able to get in and out without her hearing you. Oh, and get my hair cream out of the bathroom while you're up there. I'm gonna need it."

Elias nodded and crept through the door and up the stairs. Rick chugged the rest of his Beep as he started mentally sketching out a seduction plan for Rita MacMurphy.

"Oh, hey, Angus Junior. How did your first kiss go?" he said, only just noticing that Angus Junior had been on the front step the whole time. "Did you blow a smoke ring like I showed you?"

"Uh, not exactly." Angus Junior replied.

Rick walked down the front steps to the curb and looked up at the house. He could see Elias' mother's silhouette through the curtain of the sewing room window, humming to herself at her Singer. It would be a shame to let her go, but it was what it was.

"Smoking just isn't my thing, Rick." said Angus Junior. "I don't know what my thing is anymore. Maybe I could comfort widows like you. I've been told I'm very comforting."

"Angus me b'y," said Rick, snapping out of his daydream, "you ain't got the ass for it."

Suddenly, they heard shouting from the house.

"You had better be a ghost!" Elias' mom yelled, "Because there is no reason for my son to be here alive!"

"Mother, I abandoned ship!" Elias yelled back. "Why can't you support that?"

"Oh, the shame!" his mother shouted, "Give me that fiddle! I'm selling it, and if I can figure out how, I'm selling you!"

"Ang-Ju, catch!" Elias yelled.

He dropped Rick's jar of hair cream out of the front window. Angus Junior flinched and shielded his face as the jar shattered on the ground.

"Rick, you catch this time!" Elias yelled.

He threw his fiddle out the window and Rick caught it.

Elias' mother called out the window to him. "Rickstopher! What are you doing? Did my son put you up to this?"

"Sorry ma'am, but I've got a new business. I'm a band manager now." said Rick. "Now, get down here, Elias, me son! Let's get ye on the radio!"

"Once I tell the ladies at church group about this, you'll never work in this town again!" she yelled. "Lord, what sins have I committed? Why have you cursed me with a weird husband, a slacker son and a disloyal house boy?"

Elias slipped out the door while his mother was lamenting. She shouted at the three boys as they scampered away from the house.

But when she stopped and thought about it for a second, she realized that a life without men actually seemed pretty good.

She never saw Elias again.

8: Showcase showdown

As they swept the lobby of the Boscawen Inn, Winifred and Florence Wentzell chatted and smoked, ensuring there'd always be ash to sweep and they'd always have jobs. They were as flapper-like as you could get for young women in a town where no one had heard of jazz music yet. Basically, they wore their hair in short bobs and were drunk all the time.

"Can't believe they wouldn't give us the day off!" Winifred griped. "Best friggin' party Lunenburg's ever seen, and here we are sweeping."

"Aw, this'll cheer you up, Win," Florence said. "Check me out! I'm walkin' funny, like buddy we saw in the movies with the cane and little moustache."

Florence attempted a Charlie Chaplin impression and knocked over a mop bucket.

"Heh. Let's try and score some laudanum and go to the movies this weekend," Winifred said. "Remember the one where the French buddies fly up to the moon? Smoked 'em with a rocket right in the eye! That was jokes."

"Wouldn't really happen like that, though," Florence countered, "Moon don't got eyes."

"Art's not always realistic. Sometimes they just throw in weird stuff for fun," said Elias Waluigi Oickle, as he entered with Rick and Angus Junior. "What are you ladies sayin'?"

"Oh hey, Elias," Winifred greeted him. "You fellas got any

laudanum, by any chance?"

"Classic Win and Flo, always looking for a party," Elias said. "Well, word around town is the hardest partier this side of Cape Breton is staying here."

"Rita MacMurphy, we know. We just got around to scrubbing her puke stains out of the drapes." Florence said. "She's in room five."

"Here's the key, do whatever you want in there," Winifred said, handing it to Elias. "If anyone asks, say you threatened us for it or something."

Elias stared at them. This was the first thing that had gone right in a long time, and he wasn't quite sure how to deal with it.

"One more thing," Florence told them. "See if she's got any laudanum on her and if she'll sell us some."

"Will do! Thanks, Win, thanks, Flo," Elias said. "Well, let's get to 'er, shall we?"

He led Rick and Angus Junior down the hall as he handed Rick a scrap of paper. "Rick, when she answers the door, you say 'Special delivery' then read this brief bio. We'll come in behind you."

"Should I say who I am or why my shirt's off?" Rick asked.

"I think special delivery gets it across fine," Elias said. "Ang-Ju, I figure we'll get three songs before someone removes us from the room, so we better start playing right away. We'll open with *Enter Sandbar*, then *Mast Caress*, then, if we have time—"

"How about *Nothing Else Mackerel*?" Angus Junior suggested.

"What? We can't blow this big chance by playing some sappy ballad!" Elias snapped.

They all stopped at room five.

"Sorry, Ang-Ju, I'm just stressed," Elias backpedaled. "What I meant to say is that we should do our most polished material, and the pre-chorus of *Mackerel* still needs tightening."

He knocked on the door. "Okay, are we good? Big energy, everyone, and remember, eye contact," he whispered. "It'll be harder for her to say no if we're all looking her right in the eye the whole time."

They waited, but there was no response.

"Oh, and remember your breathing. But most of all, let's just have fun out there," he continued.

Elias knocked again, and they kept waiting.

Angus Junior breathed a sigh of relief. Since leaving the Academy, he'd been anxious about what Rita MacMurphy would say if she remembered him. "Aw jeez, I'm sorry, Elias. We ought to apologize to your mom and Hennigar and go back to our lives."

Elias unlocked the door, opened it, and peered into the room. "Looks like Rita's stuff is still here. She's probably just out getting smokes. Let's just go in and wait for her until she gets back."

He walked in, sat on the bed and started drop tuning his fiddle. "This is better, actually. It gives us a chance to rehearse."

Angus Junior and Rick followed him in.

"Ang-Ju, she'll forgive us for breaking in when she hears how good we are," Elias told him. "Now, let's do a quick run-through of *Mast Caress*. We haven't played it in a while."

Angus Junior closed the door behind him. Elias counted off, then they started playing.

"I got something to say, I killed a seagull today!" Elias sang at the top of his lungs. "And it doesn't matter much to me as long as it's dead!"

With hits like this, Rick knew he'd hitched his star to the right wagon. He began doing some kind of proto-headbanging movement, jumping around the room.

As he tooted his flute, all of Angus Junior's reservations about Jigtallica melted away. To modern ears, this music would be completely unlistenable, but to Angus Junior it felt right.

Playing this music, he felt like he belonged.

But Rita MacMurphy thought they sounded pretty stupid. She'd been hiding under the bed since she heard the knock at the door. These three young men were less threatening than the people she'd been expecting, but much more obnoxious.

She rolled out onto the floor and got to her feet. "I must insist that you dispense with the caterwauling, darlings. If you're not here to kill me, I'll simply have to ask you to leave," she said, lighting a cigarette at the end of a long holder, "I don't hold auditions in my bedroom. Too many hurt feelings, you see."

"Miss MacMurphy, it's an honour to ask what you're sayin'. We are Jigtallica and if you'll just give us a chance," Elias pleaded, "we've got the talent, we've got the drive, all we need is a break. With you behind us, we can make thrash fiddle the hot new sound of the 1920s!"

"Let me stop you right there, old sport. You've got technical chops and a certain *je ne sais quoi*, I'll give you that," she said, "but this frightful sound hasn't got appeal, darling."

Elias started to speak, but she cut him off and gestured to Angus Junior with her cigarette holder. "Plus, your husky friend here is radio poison. His charisma was positively ghastly on Kitchen Party this morning, and I simply don't give second chances. I have a reputation to protect. I'm sure you understand."

"You were on the radio this morning?" Elias asked Angus Junior. "Did you talk about the band on there?"

"Daddy humiliated him with prejudice before he could say a word, darling. Then the horrid old beast toddled to Halifax without giving me an interview. I can't believe I came all the way out to this beautiful dump for nothing." she griped.

"Ang-Ju, why didn't you tell me you were on the radio?" Elias asked, "We could've schemed something together. It could've been our big break."

"I can't imagine any scheme of yours would have worked, darling," Rita said. "Now, I am quite certain that I've asked you to leave, so if you would be so kind..."

Elias was too numb to protest. This hurt worse than losing his dad, being kicked out by his mom or having his hat slapped off by Polluto. He knew Angus Junior lacked hustle, but he didn't know he also lacked loyalty and respect.

Angus Junior felt lower than a person from Lockeport. He had just wanted to make his dad proud, but instead he hurt the only person who actually cared about him. He had to make things right with Elias, and if he could hurt his dad in the process, that would be pretty good too.

"Uh, wait!" he yelled, "You want a *Bluenose* episode? We'll give you a *Bluenose* episode."

"You have my attention, darling," Rita told him. "Let's hear your pitch, but do make it snappy."

"I'm in charge of guarding the *Bluenose* tonight," Angus Junior said. "After everyone in town's fast asleep, usually around ten, we'll sneak you onboard. You can do your show and tour the whole ship. But, you've gotta let Jigtallica play a set on air."

Rita looked at them for a moment, totally stone faced, before blowing a smoke ring. "Alright, darlings, you've got a deal," she said. "I'll let you play three songs on air, but I want something radio-friendly, nothing about killing birds or such macabre nonsense. Oh, and let's keep the banter between songs to an absolute minimum, shall we? And I want to see the *Bluenose* in action, darlings. I don't just want to bob around in Snoozenburg Harbour, I want a thrill! If she really is the fastest in the world, I want to open her up and see what she can do. These are my terms, darlings, take them or leave them."

"Deal." said Angus Junior, and shook her hand.

This was more than he had bargained for, but he was willing to do what it took to make things right with his best friend. If that meant stealing the *Bluenose,* so be it.

9: Lunenburg Mental Database (LMDb)

"What's she sayin' here?" Elias griped, pointing at Gwen.

He paced around the Lunenburg bandstand, a big gazebo in the middle of town. It had the only bench grand enough to smoke on while cooking up a scheme of this magnitude. Angus Junior, Rick, Gwen and the Wentzell sisters were gathered around him.

"Uh, I invited her," Angus Junior said. "She's got experience sailing at night."

Local superstition held that women were bad luck on ships, hence were not allowed at sea. So, for over a year, Gwen had been secretly teaching herself to pilot a ship under the cover of darkness. Normally, she would bristle at a risky proposition like this, but the odds were near certain that she'd never get the opportunity to pilot a vessel like the *Bluenose* again.

"We don't need her to tell us how to furl the sails onto the jibs or whatever. We're all perfectly capable of hoisting the...uh..." Elias trailed off.

"The *Bluenose* is a 143 foot long, 126 foot tall schooner with eight sails," Gwen informed everyone, "It sails with a crew of 20 skilled seamen."

Winifred and Florence chuckled and made hand gestures at the word 'seamen'.

"There are six of us," Gwen continued. "Assuming wind conditions are favourable, we could maybe get as far as Feltzen South. But only if everyone listens to exactly what I say. Even then, the odds of success are negligible."

"Aye aye, captain!" Angus Junior. "Right, guys?"

"Okay, fine," Elias said. "She can help. Gwen, if you want to be in charge of the boat stuff, have at 'er."

He certainly didn't care for Gwen's tone, but he didn't have much choice. In order to steal the boat, someone had to actually sail it. During his six minutes as a professional sailor, he'd been too busy getting bullied and running away to learn anything about seafaring.

"I have one condition," Gwen said. "Angus Junior's been working on a song for me. If I help, that has to be one of the songs you play on the radio."

"Oh, come on! You can't make logistical *and* creative decisions!" Elias protested.

"Elias, uh, I promise I didn't ask her to say that," Angus Junior stammered. "But playing my song isn't that big a sacrifice, is it?"

Elias closed his eyes and took a long drag on his cigarette. First Angus Junior had been keeping secrets, now his girlfriend was dictating their set list. After this show, they were going to have a serious band meeting. Members only.

"Okay, fine, whatever," he finally said. "You two can stow the mooring balls and get the sextants calibrated while you're on guard duty tonight."

"Oh, uh, well it's not just me tonight," Angus Junior said. "I'm guarding the *Bluenose*, but the wharf has its own private security."

Everyone took long, hard drags on their cigarettes. Things had been moving so fast that this was the first time anyone considered what would happen if they were caught red-handed trying to steal the *Bluenose*. To this day, it's hard to think of a more serious crime against Lunenburg.

Other towns had banished Rick for less.

"Who's on wharf duty tonight?" he asked.

"Clarence Feener," Angus Junior answered.

"We can work with that," Elias said.

From birth, every Lunenburger begins seeking out and cataloguing embarrassing stories about everyone else in town. This information is rarely used in anger, because the destruction is mutually assured: Everyone in town has a file on you, too.

There was a brief pause as everyone silently searched their Lunenburg Mental Database for dirt on 40-year-old freelance security guard Clarence Feener.

"Well, we all know ol' Clarence don't mind having a couple pops at work," Elias said, to a big round of laughs.

Clarence had been the night watchman the night before the *Bluenose* was launched. That morning, the Champagne bottle used to christen the ship was mysteriously three quarters empty. He had been busted down to part-time after that, and Captain Angus Walters always made sure his son was there to provide additional security when the *Bluenose* was in port and Feener was working.

"Flo and Win, how's your access to the Boscawen's liquor cabinet?" Elias asked.

"Unrestricted." Winifred said, and took a sip from a bottle.

"His watch doesn't start until eight, and we told Rita to meet us at ten," Angus Junior said. "Will that be enough time to get him alcoholed up?"

"Feen's a lightweight," Florence said. "I was over to a shindig with him last New Year. He had the sink clogged up with puke before midnight!"

"What a loser!" Winifred interjected, to another huge round of laughs.

"Two hours will be tight, but we can do it," Florence said, grabbing the bottle from her sister and taking a nip. "We're the best in the game, ain't we?"

"We'll show up with rum, ask him about growing up in the 90s,"

Winifred added. "Shan't be a problem after that."

Clarence was known around town for handing out flyers he'd written with titles like "Only 1890s Kids Understand Why Bikes Had A Giant Front Wheel" and "Quiz - Are You A Tesla Coil or a Ferris Wheel?"

"What a sin, those flyers," Florence said. "It's so sad that he does that."

"He's a sad lightweight to be sure, me old trouts, but don't forget the time him and Speedy was caught stealing all them buckets of frozen shrimp," Rick warned. "He ratted Speedy out right quick, and he'd squeal on us, too. Ye can't just get him a little saucy, he's gotta be lights-out."

"Okay, Rick. You and I can meet Rita at the hotel at 9:45. We'll walk her down to the waterfront, the long way. That'll buy you guys some extra time," Elias said. "Plus it'll give Rick a chance to work on his romancing, and I can maybe get some advice from her about the music industry. That work for everybody?"

Everyone nodded.

"Okay, when we show up with Rita, Feen's asleep and the *Bluenose* is ready for sail. We all get on board, Gwen sails us out to Feltzen South," Elias schemed, "Then me and Ang-Ju play our set on the radio. Rita's so impressed that she signs Jigtallica to a record deal on the spot. Rick turns on the charm during the negotiations, they get married, and we all sail home happy with new lives! Oh, Flo and Win, I didn't have a chance to ask her about laudanum, but I'm sure she's got a hookup in the city she'd put you in touch with. Sound good?"

Elias held out his hand.

"Sounds finest kind," Florence said, "I'm in." She put her hand on Elias'.

"Me too," said Winifred, "Even if we don't score any L tonight, it's still fun to get drunk on a boat." She put her hand in, too.

Rick and Angus Junior followed suit. Gwen put her hand on top, gripping Angus Junior's a little tighter than necessary. Even she was caught up in the excitement.

"Let's steal the friggin' *Bluenose*, boys!" Elias said.

Everyone raised their hands and cheered. At that moment, it all seemed possible.

~

Barely out of earshot, Schoolmaster Hennigar was at the Great War memorial, where he always went to mutter after a bad day. A sound pierced his ears that made his blood boil more than shell fire ever had: young people's laughter.

He looked over at the bandstand and studied the giggling perpetrators. It was a disgusting crew of dropouts, to be sure. Winifred and Florence Wentzell: those two were always smiling and laughing, probably at him! Rickstopher Hirtle: the degenerate out-of-towner who made his living befouling widows instead of just letting them be sad and alone like God intended! Worst of all, the ringleader, Elias Oickle, had called him out on the pee rag thing!

Those four were all beyond saving. But now they'd roped Angus Walters Junior and Gwendolyn Risser into their deviance. What were they plotting? He thought he could make out the word "Bluenose." Whatever it was, he had to put a stop to it.

A few years earlier, Hennigar had been all too ready to believe that shooting Germans in the Belgian countryside to avenge an Austrian Archduke was essential to Nova Scotia's freedom. It did not take a lot of mental gymnastics for him to convince himself that stalking these kids with a loaded rifle was the right thing to do.

10: He sings the songs that remind him of better times

That night at the Lunenburg waterfront, Angus Junior lay on the *Bluenose*'s deck and looked up at the mournful, foggy sky. Elias' grand bandstand plans, Rita MacMurphy's broadcast, Jigtallica's set and his dad's wrath all took a backseat to his broken heart.

As soon as the scheming session at the bandstand was over, Angus Junior had gone straight to the government wharf to guard the *Bluenose*, just like his dad had instructed. He knew from experience that if someone noticed he wasn't where he was supposed to be, they'd snitch on him via telegram, just for an excuse to talk to the great Captain Walters.

For hours, he sat on the deck as a steady stream of well-wishers came to see the newly-minted legend up close. Angus Junior was sweatier and more fidgety than usual, but no one noticed. The boat was the attraction, after all, not the nervous boy aboard.

Gwen was supposed to arrive at seven to start getting things ready, but she didn't show. She was the only member of the team who owned a watch, so Angus Junior knew she wasn't running late by accident. It must be personal.

By the time Clarence Feener showed up to guard the wharf at eight, Angus Junior had given up hope. The Wentzells arrived shortly thereafter with a bottle and made an offhand comment about how interesting it must have been to grow up in the 1890s. For the next hour, Feener monologued without interruption, while lovelorn Angus Junior stared out at the sea.

"Music today"—Feener scoffed, then took a swig from a mason jar full of dark rum—"Nothing like it was back in the 90s! *I've Been Workin' On The Railroad, Bicycle Built For Two, Twinkle Twinkle Little Star*...Those were all huge tunes, undeniable hits!"

"Yup, the 90s were different, alright," said Florence, feigning interest as Winifred topped up his jar. "Everyone likes hearing about that."

The plan to get the guard drunk and pass out was progressing pretty well. It was only 9 pm and he was already yelling at two young women about old music. If they could keep up this pace, the Wentzells would have him snoozing in no time.

"Music meant something back then! A song like *Happy Birthday* meant that it was somebody's birthday!" he slurred.

Angus Junior rolled his eyes. He looked away from Feener and fixated on a pile of lobster traps down the wharf. Gwen popped her head out from behind them and waved to him. She held her finger in front of her lips.

"Now, marching bands were undeniably the sound of the early 90s," Feener continued. "People had been force-fed over-produced opera music for so long. Then, boom, John Phillips Sousa comes along and just takes a wrecking ball to the whole thing."

Feener started flamboyantly marching around and playing the air sousaphone to demonstrate how he and his entire generation felt the first time they heard the *Washington Post March*.

Figuring Feener would be distracted for a while, Gwen crawled out from behind her hiding place and snuck aboard the *Bluenose* behind his back. She and Angus Junior slipped below deck to speak in private.

~

After spending their afternoon smoking cigarettes and stealing a shirt off a clothesline, Elias and Rick sat on the front stoop of the Boscawen Inn and waited for Rita.

"Elias, me son, before we do this, I gotta tell ya one thing," Rick told him, passing him one more cigarette. "If ye don't start going easier on Angus Junior, he's liable to jump ship."

"Rick, I appreciate your fatherly wisdom and what have you," Elias said. "But my mom's not a client any more. You can drop the dad act."

"I ain't talking Mom-Pleaser to Son-Figure, I'm talking as your band manager. I gotta look out for Jigtallica, long term." Rick said. "You're treating Junior like he's just a tin flute, but he ain't. He's the heart of the band. If you ain't got a good heart pumping the blood, you're gonna go limp for good. Understand?"

"After tonight, when we're big radio stars, Ang-Ju will be happy that I pushed him so far," Elias replied. "Now, let's focus. It'll be showtime any second."

Right on cue, Rita MacMurphy stepped out the front door of the hotel. Rick and Elias quickly stood up, slicked back their hair and greeted her with big smiles.

"Evening, Springtime!" Rick said. "Going my way?"

"Oh, hello again, darling," Rita replied. "I see you've beshirted yourself. I do appreciate the effort."

A hulking man with a scar on his left cheek stepped out behind her, carrying two big suitcases. "What's the big idea with these palookas?" he asked.

"Don't fret, my dear Mugsy," Rita told him. "These two strapping, young locals are here to carry the bags."

"Mugsy, is it? You must be the producer," Elias said. "There's a few things we should go over before the tech run."

"I'll ask you not to bother the help, darling," Rita cut in. "He simply twists the knobs and plugs in the cables and so on. Dreadfully banal. Now, let's be on our way, shall we?"

"Yes of course," said Elias. "We can walk and talk."

"Say, it's a nice foggy night, ain't it?" Rick mused. "How 'bout taking the long way down to the water?"

"Yeah, what's our hurry?" Elias said. "We could show you around town, fill you in on which stores and restaurants used to be different."

"Some of 'em will friggin' blow you away," Rick added.

"Here's a free lesson in etiquette, darlings," Rita said. "It's quite rude to waste the time of an urbane Haligonian such as myself. Now, the bags, darlings, the bags!"

Rita snapped her fingers and pointed at the bags. Without another word, she started briskly walking toward the waterfront, with Mugsy following close behind her.

Rick was dumbfounded that their plan to stall for time hadn't worked. No one from Lunenburg has ever considered that somebody wouldn't be interested in hearing about what their town used to be like.

Without the detour, it was barely an eight-minute walk from the Boscawen Inn to the waterfront. If Feener was still awake when they arrived, it would be game over. He'd talk Rita's ear off about his own band, Ta-Ra-Ra-Boom-De-Ay, A Tribute To The 90s, but he'd never let Jigtallica onboard the *Bluenose.*

~

The Wentzells had no way of knowing it, but their margin of error had just disappeared.

As they watched Feener's stumbling, uncoordinated march, the sisters could see their operation was nearing its endgame. When the marching ran out of steam, he sat down on the edge of the dock to catch his breath. But, as the sisters well knew, the closer he got to passing out, the more volatile he would become. From here on, they would have to act with delicate precision.

"How about a top up, there, Feen?" Florence asked, and poured him another jar of rum.

"Hmm, I should probably slow down," Feener protested. "I am at work."

"Okay, how about just a toast, then?" Winifred suggested, "To, uh..." She struggled to remember which 90s things Feener liked, and which ones he thought were overrated.

"Scott Joplin!" Florence suggested, and raised her glass.

Feener got to his feet and stared at her. "Oh, you're a big Scott Joplin fan, huh?" he said, derisively, "Name three rags!"

"Uh... Cloth?" Florence answered. "Like a cloth rag?"

"You wanna hear the real truth about Scott Joplin? Angus Junior should hear this, too. It's important!" Feener shouted. "Angus Junior, listen to this!"

Clarence looked up at the *Bluenose*, but didn't see Angus Junior on deck. "Where is he?"

"Who cares?" Winifred said, "Hey, uh... Airplanes got invented in the 90s right? Why don't you tell us about that?"

"What? No, that was the mid 00s!" Feener scoffed. "Haven't you been listening?"

Reminiscing about the 90s had been as intoxicating as the rum itself and Clarence Feener had gotten carried away. In a moment of clarity, he remembered that the Wentzell sisters had gotten three night watchmen in town drunk before as part of three separate heists.

He looked down at his jar of rum and sighed. "Are you trying to get me drunk for a heist?"

"What? No, we're just having fun, spinning yarns!" Winifred protested.

"Yeah! How about you tell us again about how guys used to have big moustaches?" Florence asked. "Or how ladies used to wear puffy sleeves?"

"No! You young people don't really care about the 90s like I do! You only like the fashion!" Feener yelled. "It was about more than just shirtwaists and sailor suits! You don't get it and you never will!"

"Maybe you better lay down and rest your eyes for a sec," Winifred suggested, "You've got the spins some bad."

The spins were coming on strong indeed, but the crisp sea air and a newfound sense of purpose helped Feener rally. He poured his drink into the ocean and confidently stumbled up the wharf and climbed aboard the *Bluenose*.

"Angus Junior! Where are you?" he shouted. "Whatever you kids are planning, I'm putting a stop to it!"

As they said in the 90s, everything was going great...Not!

11: Gwen calls the heart

Below deck on the *Bluenose*, Angus Junior and Gwen sat next to each other on the edge of Angus Senior's berth.

"Hey, uh, happy you made it. So, uh, did you go to the wrong wharf earlier, or...?" Angus Junior asked. "Not that it's a big deal that you're a bit late or whatever, I just—"

"I came here to apologize," Gwen said softly. "I can't pilot this vessel with you tonight."

Angus Junior wasn't sure if this was better or worse than being stood up. Rather than consider it, he talked quickly to fill the silence. "Oh, uh, I accept your apology, don't even worry about it. A schooner like this is pretty intimidating, I get it. Can you just show me how to get the sails up and pointed in the right direction? I'll figure it out from there. And then maybe I'll see you at the fish stand tomorrow?"

"I'm not intimidated by the boat. I said I couldn't pilot this vessel with you."

"Oh, uh..." said Angus Junior. This was much worse.

He got up to his feet. "I get it. Totally fine. I'm just, uh, gonna go maybe have a drink with Feener and them. My eyes are feeling a little seasick, that's why they're watery."

"Angus Junior, wait!" Gwen put her hand on his shoulder. She took a device from her pocket and showed it to him.

"Uh, is your watch broken?" he asked.

"It's a barometer," she explained. "It's moving that way because the wind conditions are unstable. To navigate a vessel through seas like this, you need to constantly reevaluate your situation and adjust. But when I'm around you…I don't know why, but my ability to assess risk is greatly diminished."

"Oh, uh, well… Sorry, I didn't know I was doing that," he said.

Gwen put down her pocket barometer and stepped closer to Angus Junior. "Sometimes when I'm with you, I don't fear uncertainty," she said. "I welcome it to a certain degree."

"Oh, uh, I'm your guy, then," Angus Junior said. "I'm very uncertain!"

Before things could escalate, Feener climbed down the ladder.

"Aha!" he yelled. "Are you kids monkeying around with the instruments down here? I knew something was up! You two wait here. I'm going to telegraph your dad!"

"You mean telephone?" Angus Junior asked.

"No, telegraph!" Feener said, already part-way up the ladder. "You know, the little finger click and beep machine you use to send a message. Sorry to break it to you kids, but not everything is about phones!"

~

Rita and Mugsy walked across Pelham Street at a quick, big-city tempo. As lifelong small-towners, Rick and Elias already had a biological aversion to walking at a reasonable pace, but tonight they walked even slower on purpose. Every moment they dawdled was extra time for the Wentzells to complete their important drinking work.

"We're about halfway, how about we take a smoke break?" Elias asked the group. "Rick, can I skeeze one?"

"I'll thank you to keep pace, darlings!" Rita called. "Smoke 'em walking. It's not polite to keep a lady waiting."

"Yeah, and go easy with those bags, you milksops!" Mugsy insisted. "I got diodes and antennas in there, see?"

Rick took a long look at Mugsy as he lit a cigarette. "Don't I know you from somewheres?" he asked. "Did you ever work the widow angle in Shelburne County?"

"No, no, you got me all wrong, see? I never worked an angle in my life!" Mugsy insisted. "I'm a radio producer, in Bedford, see? It's a traditional stopping place, see? You must've stopped in and seen me around some time! Yeah, that's it."

"Is that right?" Rick said, unconvinced.

"What's the music scene like in Bedford?" Elias asked. "Is it pretty easy to get booked, or do you have to know somebody?"

"Oh, do shut up, darling!" Rita said. "I've asked you nicely not to speak to him, and I simply haven't the patience to bear this any longer. In the business of show, things operate according to a schedule. They do not operate according to the whims of a couple of wretched street waifs! Are we recording a radio programme from the *Bluenose* tonight, or are we not?"

"Uh, we are," Elias said, with Angus Junior-like uncertainty.

"Then I suggest, darling, that you start moving your gams and stop flapping your gums. I'm the only one who should be flapping around here, because I'm a flapper," Rita said. "Now flap this: If tonight is anything short of perfectly marvellous, I will use the full weight of my fabulous prestige to destroy your musical career before it even begins. I'll have you positively blackballed off of every stage from here to Prince Edward Island. Now, I trust there will be no further delays, yes?"

Elias did what anyone starting out in show business would do and took an established person's verbal abuse with good humour. "Right this way, ma'am," he said, and hoped the Wentzells were ahead of schedule.

~

They weren't. Back at the waterfront, the Wentzell sisters were pleading with Feener not to rat them out with his dated 90s technology.

"Come on Feen, aren't we having a good time?" Florence pleaded.

"At least have another drink or two before you snitch," Winifred suggested.

"Out of my way, ladies" Feener said. "I have clicks to beep."

He climbed off the *Bluenose* and started stumbling down the wharf.

"Feener, wait!" Angus Junior called. "I swear we're not doing anything with my dad's boat! We were just, uh…"

Feener looked back and saw Angus Junior and Gwen standing together in the moonlight. He had a keen memory for the pop culture of his teenage years but had forgotten what being young really felt like. It slowly dawned on him that a teenage couple might want to monkey around with something other than nautical instruments.

"Wait, were you two about to French kiss in there?" he asked them.

"Uh…" Angus Junior answered, looking over at Gwen.

"Matters of the heart are notoriously difficult to forecast, Mr. Feener," Gwen answered, "but if I had to give a rough estimate, I would put the chances of us frenching at three in five."

"Angus Junior, you little scamp!" Feener said. "If you had told me you were getting a little seaside smooch tonight, I wouldn't have tried to stop you. I'm not a prude like William Jennings Bryan or something!"

"I'm sorry, who?" asked Angus Junior.

"You know, William Jennings Bryan! The religious guy who ran for president in the 90s? You seriously don't know who that is? God, I feel old," Feener rambled on. "Anyway, my point is, if you wanted some time alone, you guys didn't need to get me this slam jammed. I can barely stand up right now."

"We're sorry, Feen," Florence said. "It was the only way we knew how."

"Please, accept our apology toast," Winifred said, solemnly raising a jar.

Feener followed suit and, as he took one last swig, his rally came to an end.

"You know what? This was the most fun I've had in a while. I needed a night like this." He yawned. "I'm just gonna lay down for a minute. Wake me up when everybody's done frenching."

He lay down on a pile of ropes and pulled a net over himself like a blanket. "How can they not know WJB?" he muttered to himself as he sank into a deep sleep. "It was a perfect reference."

Florence squatted and snapped her fingers in his face, making sure he was asleep. "Phew, he's out," she said, then lit a cigarette. "Holy Jumpins, he must've had a full stomach."

"I never doubted us for a second," said Winifred, using Florence's cherry to light a smoke of her own.

"Is he okay?" called Angus Junior.

"Oh yeah, he'll be fine," Winifred said. "He's known for this sort of thing."

Just then, Rita MacMurphy arrived with her entourage.

"What are you guys sayin'?" Elias asked the Wentzells.

"Not much, just put Feen down for his nap," Florence answered. "You guys got here some quick."

"Well, you know what they say," Elias said. "In the business of show, things operate according to a schedule."

Florence and Winifred rolled their eyes.

Elias led Rita down the wharf to the *Bluenose*. "Right this way,

Miss MacMurphy. I believe you've already met our crew, except for Gwen. She's in charge of the nuts and bolts of the boating stuff."

Gwen and Angus Junior waved from on deck.

"Charmed, I'm sure," Rita said. "How soon do we set sail, darlings? I'm simply dying to get this over with."

"I'm sure we'll be ready in no time," said Elias. "They've been prepping the boat all afternoon. Isn't that right?"

Getting pressured into things was part of being friends with Elias. Angus Junior knew this and accepted it, but he wasn't about to let him do the same thing to Gwen. "Uh...actually," he said, "Gwen says she's not gonna—"

"We're just waiting for the fog to clear and then we'll be on our way," Gwen butted in. "Miss MacMurphy, please make yourself comfortable on board."

"Uh, what? Are you sure about this?" Angus Junior asked her.

"As a good forecaster, I'm never totally sure," Gwen answered. "I deal in probabilities, and it is highly probable that I want to hear your mackerel song tonight."

"Okay great!" Elias said. "Let's get this show on the sea!"

A proper navigator revises their forecast based on new data, and data had been coming in hard and fast since Gwen arrived at the wharf. All day long, she'd put the odds of this caper going catastrophically wrong at around 80%, which still held firm. However, the chance that she would regret missing out on this for the rest of her life was 85%. That afternoon, it had only been 50%, but the feeling she got when she actually stood aboard the *Bluenose* moved it up 5%, and her close brush with frenching below deck had moved it up another 10%. When Angus Junior started standing up for her, the needle moved 20%.

Under these circumstances, helping a cute boy steal the world's fastest boat was the rational choice.

12: The unintended consequences of the Treaty of Versailles

For years, School Master Hennigar had been complaining that the Treaty of Versailles was too soft on teens. If juvenile delinquent Gavrilo Princip had gotten the proper discipline in school, he never would have fallen in with a bad crowd. He never would have shot Archduke Franz Ferdinand while showing off for his friends, and the Great War wouldn't have happened. The Armistice should have reflected that, and an international league should have been formed to stamp out Smart Aleckyness across the globe.

Justifiably, no one had listened to him. But now Hennigar had a chance to prove himself right. The *Bluenose* was such a powerful symbol, if he could catch these punks defiling it, Lunenburg town council might finally step up where the diplomats of 1919 had failed and lay down the law. Surely the world would follow suit.

He wasn't history's worst lunatic with a Treaty of Versailles-related chip on his shoulder, but he was still pretty bad.

After Elias and his belligerent band of ne'er-do-wells left the bandstand, Hennigar spent the rest of his day waiting for the cover of darkness. He had to be stealthy to catch them red-handed. If they saw him coming, they'd disperse or, worse, call him a perv.

As he did every day, he spent the afternoon doing push ups in a dimly-lit room, then ate a boiled potato for supper while cleaning his service rifle. Usually he only affixed the bayonet on weekends, but tonight he treated himself.

When night fell, he marched down Hopson Street, whistling *It's a Long Way to Tipperary*, rifle fully cocked and loaded. For a public school employee in Lunenburg County, none of this was strange behaviour.

~

Rick, Elias and the Wentzell sisters smoked cigarettes on the bow of the *Bluenose* and blankly stared at Gwen.

"Alright everyone, the tide is moving with the wind," she explained, "so we're gonna set the gaff, mainsail and mizzen, but wait until my signal to hoist the jib."

Everyone stared in a stunned silence for a moment.

"I'll hoist your jib!" Florence finally yelled.

Winifred laughed. "Set my gaff while you're at it!"

"Okay, good, you understand," Gwen answered. "Communication is absolutely crucial, so I just want to go over the—"

"Gwen, we get it," Elias said. "I'm sure we'll be fine. Now come on, let's get moving before someone sees us. Ang-Ju, how's that knot coming along?"

Angus Junior was sitting on the wharf, struggling in vain to untie the rope that moored the *Bluenose*. "Uh, getting close, I think!" he shouted back.

"Okay great," Elias said, and walked away from Gwen. "Did you hear that, Miss MacMurphy? We're just about ready to launch. So, for the show tonight, how much time are you doing off the top?"

"Hold it right there!" barked a distant voice.

Angus Junior dropped the rope and put his hands in the air.

Schoolmaster Hennigar marched down the wharf with his rifle pointed at Elias. "Disembark from that vessel, all of you!" he ordered.

Elias rolled his eyes. If something was going to derail his master plan, it wasn't going to be this guy. "Go about your business every-body," he said. "He pulls guns on people all the time. It's fine."

"You're all under citizen's arrest," said Hennigar. "Except Gwen and Angus Junior. You two are on citizen's probation."

"What?" yelled Florence. "That is so unfair!"

"We wasn't even doin' nothin'!" said Winifred.

"Yeah!" Florence added. "We're just standing on a boat. That ain't illegal, is it?"

"Yes, it is!" yelled Hennigar. "It's not your boat!"

"We're from Lunenburg, ain't we?" Winifred replied. "The *Bluenose* belongs to all of us, don't it?"

This sounded too much like socialism for Hennigar to listen any further. But he had to concede, they'd inadvertently raised a good point. The *Bluenose* was moored. Hennigar couldn't really prove they were trying to steal anything.

He'd reported so many teenage misdemeanours over the years that the local police had politely thanked him for his military service, then firmly asked him to stop. If he wanted to use this incident to justify a campaign of brutal revenge on the local youth, he was going to have to sell it.

Hennigar cautiously stepped aboard the ship. He kept his rifle trained on Elias, who was standing beneath the mainsail.

"Hoist the sail!" Hennigar ordered.

The tip of his bayonet touched Elias' throat. As far as throat-cutting was concerned, Hennigar was no Polluto, but he seemed to know what he was doing.

For the first time that day, Elias did as he was told. "Fine. But I was gonna do it anyway!"

He pulled the rope, unfurling the mainsail. It started filling with wind, lurching the *Bluenose* forward. Soon, the only thing keeping the wind from carrying her out of the harbour was the knot that Angus Junior had barely loosened.

Now Hennigar had evidence. Anyone could plainly see that Elias was trying to steal the *Bluenose*, and in Lunenburg this was grounds for justifiable homicide.

"Mugsy, my good man, do subdue this unhinged beast, won't you?" Rita said. "His crazed shouting and urine scent are putting me dreadfully ill at ease."

Mugsy opened one of his suitcases and took out a Tommy gun. "86 the heater, see?" he said, pointing the gun at Hennigar.

Hennigar wasn't familiar enough with prohibition-era gangster-speak to totally understand what he was being asked. But one thing was clear: in the deadliest pact since Austria-Hungary and Germany, the teens had formed an alliance with people from out of town.

Now that he truly understood what he was up against, no tactic would be off the table. "You'll all burn for this!" he yelled, just before Mugsy gunbutted him in the forehead and knocked him out.

"Thank you, darling!" Rita said. "Now, children, if there are no more wretched men to incapacitate, I suggest we set sail."

For a moment, no one was quite sure what to do. They couldn't deny that Hennigar had been the aggressor here, and that it was good that he'd been subdued. However, no one was exactly happy about the escalating gun-butt play.

Elias sensed the tension in the air. His radio debut was too close at hand for him to give up now, just because everyone had mixed feelings about assaulting a teacher. He had to act fast before people had a chance to think twice.

"Ang-Ju! Hop on, buddy!" he yelled, winking as he added, "Trust me."

Angus Junior scrambled aboard as Elias picked up Hennigar's rifle and used the bayonet to slice through the knot that he'd 'almost untied'.

The *Bluenose* was no longer tied to Lunenburg, and a gust of wind blew the schooner away from the dock. Now she was bound only to the will of the tide, the wind, and a fifteen-year-old with a few months of self-taught sailing experience.

13: Elias takes everyone for granted

As the *Bluenose* began her voyage, Florence leaned against the bowsprit (the long pole that sticks out of the front of a ship) and thrust her hips forward.

"Check me out," she yelled. "Looks like I got a big long wanger, eh?"

"Careful up there!" Gwen yelled.

"Don't be a party poop deck, Gwen," said Elias. "She's just having fun."

Quicker than you could slit a fish throat, the voyage had changed from a light-hearted romp to the violent kidnapping of a decorated war veteran. As the *Bluenose* entered the open ocean, Elias was desperate to revive the party atmosphere.

"Fun is ill-advised right now! I need you all to listen very carefully," Gwen said.

"Gwen, relax!" Elias protested. "We're way out in the ocean. What are we gonna crash into? It's just water out here. Besides—"

There was a loud crack of thunder. Rain fell, wind blew and waves crashed. The ocean tossed the *Bluenose* around like a toddler trying to keep a balloon off the floor.

Gwen frantically shouted commands, but it was no use.

Because everyone aboard had grown up in age-of-sail Nova Scotia, Gwen had thought at least one of them would know something about sailing. But the "crew" she commanded didn't know a slip from a sloop. She would have to do it all herself.

She had taught herself to sail on a ship about an eighth of the *Bluenose*'s size, with only one sail. But for the next twenty minutes, she ran around the schooner and kept it afloat until the wind and waves calmed down.

When the sea was finally still, everyone politely applauded.

Now that Gwen had steered them through the rough weather, Elias knew that if he didn't act fast, everyone was liable to start listening to her instead of him. And just like Angus Junior, she was sure to cut and run on Jigtallica as soon as the going got tough.

"Let's keep that applause going for Gwen, everybody!" he said. "And give yourselves a round, too. It was rough out there, but we really all came together. Obviously, I'm happy with whatever everybody else wants to do next. But since we're out here and the sea's calmed down, how about we tie up Hennigar, put him below deck, and then get the radio show started? It would be a shame to have gone through all that for nothing, right?"

Fog was starting to close in, making it hard to tell where they were or in which direction they were headed. Gwen knew the only sensible course of action was to navigate back to a safe harbour immediately. But she had learned that this crew did not respond to orders. She decided to copy Elias' strategy of pretending to be laid back instead of just directly saying what she wanted.

"Hmm, that's one idea for sure," she said. "No pressure or anything, but maybe we could also think about navigating home while the weather is cooperating."

"No pressure from me, either. I'm cool with whatever we decide," said Elias. "I guess what I'm saying is that we might want to make sure Hennigar can't stab or shoot us when he wakes up. But we certainly don't have to. We can do Gwen's idea instead."

"I never said we shouldn't tie him up," Gwen said.

"Okay, great. Then it sounds like we all agree," Elias said. "Rick and I will tie Hennigar up, and while we do, these guys set up their radio equipment. That way if we do decide to do the show, we've got our bases covered. It pays to be prepared, right, Gwen?"

"I'm fine either way," Gwen answered through gritted teeth, "but just letting you guys know, things get more dangerous the longer we stay out here. Not that it's a big deal."

"I totally hear you," said Elias. "Which is why, instead of a full rehearsal, Ang-Ju and I will just do a cue to cue tech run. We can play the rest of the timing details by ear. Sounds like we've got a plan we can all live with. What do you think, Ang-Ju? It's your dad's boat, after all."

"Uh...Yeah, I guess that sounds okay." Angus Junior replied. "If everybody's happy with that."

"I could go for tying Hennigar up," said Rick after a long pause. "If that's what we're doing."

The Wentzell sisters nodded in agreement.

"Okay great!" Elias said. "We'll get on that while Mugsy sets up the radio antenna and Miss MacMurphy does her vocal warmups. Then put on a tight thirty-minute show and head back. Everybody wins! This is still gonna be a fun night, I think."

~

"Okay, pass him down!" Rick yelled from the *Bluenose*'s sleeping quarters, below deck.

Elias dropped Hennigar head-first down the companionway. But Rick was too deep in thought to catch him in time and his head thudded on the wooden floor.

"Ah well," Elias muttered. "I guess that's payback for the year he gave out math homework over Christmas break."

He climbed down after Hennigar and helped Rick lift him onto one of the bunks. "Thanks again, Rick," he grunted. "Other than some navigation issues on Gwen's part, I think the plan is going pretty much perfectly so far."

Rick shook his head as he tied Hennigar's wrists to the bunk. "Elias, me son, I'm warning ye. Don't get so pleased with the sound of a woman's moans that you can't hear her husband's footsteps coming up the stairs. Understand?"

"No. You need a new frame of reference."

"I mean watch your back around these city folk. They ain't to be trusted."

"Let's not write them off just yet. It's not like they're from Lockeport or something," Elias responded.

"They's hiding something from us," Rick said. "What's Mugsy got a gun like that for? Shooting birds that block the radio waves?"

"Maybe! I don't know how radio works, do you? Why is it normal for a school principal to have a gun, but suspicious for a radio producer?"

"I don't think he's a radio producer!" Rick snapped. "I know for sure he ain't from Bedford!"

"How do you know?"

Rick paused. Elias saw a brief flash of fear in Rick that he never had before, as if he'd said too much.

"I can't tell you," Rick stammered. "You just have to trust me."

"You're keeping secrets now? Without ever being asked, you've told me about the pubic hair length of half the women in town. What could possibly be so private that you can't tell me?"

Rick looked away.

"Elias!" Florence shouted from above. "Get up here!"

"Just a second!" Elias yelled back. "Rick, I gotta go. Can you gag Hennigar without me? Look, if you don't trust that Mugsy guy, I don't trust him, either. Once we're back in Lunenburg, we'll get a crew together and beat him up. Sound good?"

"Elias!" Winifred shouted. "Hurry!"

"Sound good?" Elias repeated, already climbing up the ladder.

"Yeah, sounds good."

Rick sighed, and muttered to himself as he put a gag in Hennigar's mouth and finished tying him up.

~

"Quit trying to mooch our booze, Miss Priss!" Florence yelled at Rita. "You can afford your own!"

"Yeah!" Winifred agreed. "We didn't drink Feen under the table just to spend the night not drinking!"

Rita waved Elias over as he climbed up on deck. "Elias, darling. Explain to these flapper-lites that a quart of rum is in my rider."

"Win, Flo, I've got a lot on my plate here," Elias pleaded. "Can't you just share for tonight?"

"Share a bottle, Elias?" Florence asked. "In the middle of a pandemic?"

"Spanish Flu ended a year ago!" he said.

"Did it? Or did we all just stop caring?" asked Winifred. Back in '22, it was still too soon to think about that sort of thing.

"You two never cared about Spanish Flu," Elias protested. "At the height of it, you ran a kissing booth!"

"To raise money for a cure!" Florence yelled.

"Besides, that ain't the issue," Winifred added. "Issue is, she can't do whatever she wants just 'cause she's famous."

"I'm not saying she can do whatever she wants just because she's famous," Elias said. "I'm saying she can do whatever she wants because she can help me."

"This is typical," Winifred scoffed. "A fancy lady from Halifax comes into town, and Elias is on her side."

"He's gone Hali!" Florence said.

"He has gone Hali!" Winifred echoed. "Come on, Flo. Let's go downstairs and drink with Rick and the tied-up chummy there. At least we know where they stand."

"Okay, but be back up here when the show starts," Elias shouted to them as they stormed off. "I want it to sound like we've got a big crowd on the radio!"

~

Angus Junior and Gwen stood at the helm, gazing into the sky. While Gwen searched for breaks in the fog or any hint of their location, Angus Junior watched Mugsy install a small radio antenna on top of a mast.

Angus Junior had known from the beginning that they were going to get caught. Getting caught was part of the fun. All afternoon he had fantasized about saying to his dad with Elias-like confidence, "Hey old man, I stole your precious *Bluenose*, and I sailed it just as good as you! You're not so great!"

Getting caught stealing the *Bluenose* was one thing, getting caught sinking it was quite another. And it was starting to feel very possible. There were simmering tensions and dangerous guns onboard. The weather was unstable and unpredictable, and now a stranger was crawling around the rigging, hooking up a lightning rod.

Elias approached. "Mind if I borrow Ang-Ju for a moment? Or should I say, Captain Ang-Ju? Cap-Ju?"

Gwen just sighed.

Elias put his arm around Angus Junior's shoulder and started nervously pacing the deck with him. "Okay, so Rita seems pretty tired and irritated. Good news, she probably won't do too much time off the top. Bad news, she'll be tougher to impress, so we gotta keep it tight." he said, all in one breath. "Just a few things before we go on. *Master Of Poopdecks*: don't forget, we added that second solo. *Mast Caress*: remember, tempo, tempo, tempo. As for

Mackerel, I think deep down we both know—"

"Look," Angus Junior interrupted, "I think maybe Gwen was right. Maybe we should delay the set until we get back to Lunenburg."

"Cap-Ju, we have to do it now," Elias insisted. "When Gwen hears your world-class tin fluting, her stress about being lost in the fog will melt away and she'll be able to navigate better. Don't you want to help her out?"

"Uh..."

"But I hear your concerns, and I agree that we should get back to land sooner than later. So, in the spirit of compromise, let's shorten our set and cut a song."

Before Angus Junior could say "Uh..." again, Rita MacMurphy approached.

"We're skipping the sound check, darlings. Just don't get too close to the microphone and you'll be fine. Now, what is the name of your ridiculous little band again?"

"Jigtallica," Elias told her.

"Yes, of course. How are all the wires and doodads looking, Mugsy?"

"Swell, see?" Mugsy replied.

"Alright, let's get this over with, shall we?" Rita told Elias. "You're on in ten, I trust you're prepared."

"Absolutely!"

She dismissed them with a royal-family wave of the hand and went over to commune with the microphone.

"Are you excited or what, Ang-Ju? Oh, *Nothing Else Mackerel* is the one we're cutting, right? I don't see any other options."

"Why that one?"

"Ang-Ju, come on," Elias said. "We only get one chance to make a first impression. When we get a record deal, I promise it'll be one of our first B sides. Anyway, I should make sure all that sloshing around didn't knock my fiddle out of tune. We can do this, buddy. We got this!"

Angus Junior had never had a best friend or a girlfriend before, and it was becoming clear that he couldn't have both at once. He would have to choose between them, and for many obvious reasons, he was leaning towards Gwen.

Even if the *Bluenose* somehow made it safely back to Lunenburg, there was no avoiding the emotional shipwreck on the horizon.

14: Jigtallica's big break

Rita MacMurphy stood in front of a microphone at the bow of the Bluenose. Mugsy fiddled with some knobs and dials until everything was to his satisfaction. He gave Rita the thumbs-up and thus began the defining moment of Jigtallica's career.

"Ladies and gentlemen, I'm Rita MacMurphy and welcome once again to my kitchen party," Rita said. "I'm coming to you live from the fabulous *Bluenose*, where we are aimlessly drifting the sea at the whim of some ragged guttersnipes."

"Woo!" Florence cheered.

Waiting for his cue, Elias was engaged in his pre-show ritual, frantically pacing in tight circles, chain smoking and muttering at Angus Junior.

No musician from Lunenburg had ever played a show on the radio before. It was the biggest musical opportunity this town would see until 1993, when the guy from Len produced an alt-rock EP by the local optometrist's three sons.

"Again, big energy out there!" Elias said. "We want to sound like we're having fun, but not so much fun that we won't get taken seriously. Oh! I was thinking for the intro, the show is called 'Kitchen Party', how about we say something like we're the table? You know, we're central to the whole thing. Or the stove maybe, because we're hot."

"Sure," said Angus Junior. "Either is fine."

~

It had been getting hard for Angus Junior to remember why he'd ever been excited about Jigtallica in the first place. Usually, when Elias was getting to be a bit much, Angus Junior would think about a big reaction they'd gotten from a crowd or an exciting riff they were working on and he'd come back around. But tonight, these weren't the moments that came to mind.

The trouble was there from Jigtallica's founding. Days after their improvised jam session at the *Bluenose* launch party, Elias was waiting at the Lunenburg Academy steps when Angus Junior got out of class.

"Ang-Ju, there he is! What are you sayin', bud?" Elias greeted him. "I have been looking for you all over town. It didn't even occur to me that someone who plays such hard music would go to school."

"Oh, hey," said Angus Junior. "I do go to school, yeah."

"Weird. Hey, I just quit The Diddlin' Fiddlers. I've gone as far as I can with them, you know? I can't stop thinking about *Sea and Destroy*. Do you wanna start a band?"

It was the first time anyone had offered to spend their free time with Angus Junior. "Uh...sure, yeah. That could be fun."

"Great!" Elias said. "Ang-Ju, you're a pip, ya know that? Rehearsals start tomorrow. I've got us booked on a variety show at the Legion this Tuesday. For the band name, I'm thinking something like Jigadeth."

This was the baseline amount of pressure that Elias would put on Angus Junior. It had steadily been ratcheting up ever since.

"Ladies and gentlemen, please welcome a band that I think will be memorable in some way, Jigtronica!" Rita MacMurphy announced, to a smattering of applause.

Staring off into the fog, Angus Junior nearly missed their cue.

Elias nudged him. Absolutely typical, he thought. Jigtallica was about to address the entire world, and Angus Junior was off looking for Lunenburg. So much talent, so little vision.

He approached the mic. "What are you sayin', world? We are Jigtallica. If you want a kitchen party, you got the right guys!"

"Uh, because we are the table!" Angus Junior said. "Or, uh, the stove, maybe."

It didn't land because Angus Junior hadn't rehearsed it. Typical. He never rehearsed hard enough, never wanted it bad enough. He still hadn't even dropped out of school.

Elias had dragged Angus Junior kicking and screaming into every opportunity so far. How would he act in a recording studio, or on a tour? He didn't have the big time mentality, and Elias was starting to worry that he never would.

Elias tapped his bow against his fiddle to count off, and then launched into *Master Of Poopdecks*. By now the fog was so thick that Angus Junior could barely see him, let alone the audience. Classic Elias: playing into the void for no one but himself.

Angus Junior stoically tooted his flute for seven and a half more minutes, until the song ended to polite applause. He was technically proficient, but did not bring the 'big energy' that Elias had asked for.

After the song, Elias immediately stood in front of the microphone, blocking Angus Junior's access. After the botched intro, he'd lost banter privileges. "How's everybody doing? I just want to clarify what my friend said earlier about us being a table…"

Angus Junior drifted off again.

Since that first day, every afternoon he and Elias would walk together from the Lunenburg Academy to their jam space in Angus Junior's root cellar. On their way, they'd pass by Risser's Fish Market. On days when her brothers were out fishing, Gwendolyn Risser worked the counter.

One day as they passed, Elias noticed Angus Junior slowing down to scope out his crush.

"I'm trying to come up with ideas for songs about battles and stuff, and you're not paying attention!" Elias told him. "If you like her so much, go order some mackerel or something."

"I don't know if that's such a good idea," Angus Junior demurred.

"I don't see the big deal here. Last night you rocked the New Germany church hall harder than they've ever been rocked before. I think you can chat up a fishmonger."

"Don't call her that, she's not a monger!"

"I'm pretty sure 'monger' is the correct term," Elias said. "She's selling, or 'monging', fish, isn't she? Now, get out there and mong yourself!"

He pushed Angus Junior into the line.

"Next!" yelled Gwen.

Angus Junior nervously approached. "Uh…" he stammered. "I'll have one, uh…mackerel."

"Anything else?" Gwen asked.

He wasn't prepared for this. Should he order something else? What kind of guy just orders one mackerel? She was gonna think he was obsessed with mackerel. Then again, would buying an additional cod seem normal?

"Nothing else!" he blurted.

She handed him his fish.

"Mackerel!" he repeated, then left.

In the coming months, Gwen and Angus Junior would grow more comfortable, and "Nothing Else, Mackerel!" would become an inside joke between them. He even wrote it into a song for her. One that Elias had cut from every set. He always had a new excuse, but Angus Junior knew the real reason. His relationship with Gwen was something Elias couldn't control, and he couldn't stand that.

"Okay, this next one is actually a mix of two song ideas. One about burning to death and another one about drowning under ice," Elias told the microphone. "We couldn't decide which was scarier, so we included both."

Before he could finish, Angus Junior started playing a soft and slow tune. This time he was the one taking action. The one changing things on the fly to suit his needs. He was going to play *Nothing Else Mackerel* on the radio, and there was nothing Elias could do about it.

Elias was uncharacteristically at a loss for words. Angus Junior was playing that ballad of his, and he had a look in his eye that Elias had never seen. It was good to finally see that spark, but why did it have to be for such a generic-sounding slow number?

Elias had no choice but to play along and hope for the best. Rita MacMurphy would not forgive an on-air blow up. He kept time by slowly knocking on his fiddle like a bongo drum, hoping this would disguise the fact that he did not know the tune.

After a few measures, Angus Junior gestured to Elias. He must be missing his vocal cue.

He cleared his throat at the microphone, but no words came. "Uh, this one's in Gaelic," he said, then improvised a guttural moan. "Da-boom-gah-gah-mmm-gah-gah-na-ee-mah! Go!"

Then he tried to salvage the situation the only way he knew how, with a long, improvised fiddle solo.

"Oh, this is the song?" Gwen asked aloud. "Hmm. It's less impressive than I had predicted."

As Elias ripped the wickedest solo he could, all the rage Angus Junior had been suppressing for months came loose. Playing this song was the only thing he'd ever asked of Elias, and he hadn't even learned the words.

He dropped his tin flute, walked over to Elias and sucker-punched him right in the mouth. Elias dropped his fiddle and fell flat on his back.

Rita MacMurphy stepped forward to break it up, but Rick got in her way. "Let them go," he said. "This here's been a long time coming."

Angus Junior sat on Elias' chest and grabbed him by the shirt collar.

"What is wrong with you, Ang-Ju?" Elias yelled.

"What's wrong with you? You couldn't sing my song one time?"

"Yeah, I forgot some of the words! So what? You were so busy with your fishmonger girlfriend all day that we didn't have time to rehearse!" Elias answered. "Now, get off of me!"

"I memorized every single one of your songs about wizards and dragons!" Angus Junior yelled, shaking him. "You can't learn one of mine?"

This was the first time Angus Junior had ever stood up for himself, but he simply did not have the follow-through to win a fight.

Elias grappled his way on top of him. "I quit Tommy Diddler and his Diddlin' Fiddlers so I wouldn't have to learn this kind of boring song anymore! We're pioneering a new sound here, not playing lazy ballads about ordering fish!"

"You're no pioneer," Angus Junior scoffed. "You're just a no-talent fiddler with a chip on his shoulder. No matter how much you scheme, you don't have the talent to make it! Thrash fiddle doesn't have broad appeal! It's niche!"

Elias had never heard such hurtful words. He felt well within his rights to fill Angus Junior in with punches. But by now, the fog had cleared just enough that Elias could see everyone had gathered around, and the crowd was not on his side.

"You know what? You're not even worth it," he said, standing up. "I made you, Ang-Ju! You wouldn't have any friends if I didn't make you get up on stage. You would have never even met Gwen if I didn't push you into the fish line. After she breaks up with you and you're back in your dad's shadow with no friends, don't come crawling back to me!"

He walked away and looked for a place to sulk, while Gwen rushed to Angus Junior and helped him up.

Rita MacMurphy approached the microphone. "Let's hear it for Jigtera. Passionate young men, to be sure," she said. "I'd like to slow things down a little bit with this next one, darlings. It's a song from the old country about a little girl whose father goes to sea to search for Potato Island."

The haunting sound of Rita MacMurphy singing in actual Gaelic filled the *Bluenose*.

Elias leaned against a rail, stared at the ocean and lit one of Rick's cigarettes. All his schemes, hustles and striving had come to an end. Just like his father, his dreams had sunk in the Atlantic, somewhere off Nova Scotia's southern coast.

Jigtallica was dead.

15: Ahoy, Darlings!

Like all Nova Scotian celebrities from the early 20th century, Rita MacMurphy has mostly been forgotten today. But she wasn't just a radio host. In her very specific time and place, she was a cultural force, dominating nearly every aspect of Scotial media.

She was born in 1886 to seamstress Agnes MacMurphapopolus and popular Queen Victoria impersonator Razzekiel Dazzleman. She was tap-dancing alongside her father on the Maritime cabaret circuit by the time she could walk. By age ten, she had played all the major markets from Edmunston to Charlottetown, and opened for legendary talents like comedian Newfie Ned and crooner Fishstick McGlick.

At fifteen, she struck out on her own as an actress, and starred in Nova Scotia's first hit motion picture, 1901's *Girl Enters and Exits Building*.

By the time she was tapped to host Kitchen Party, she was already a household name in the Maritime provinces. She boasted impressive phonograph sales, and her nightlife column 'Ahoy, Darlings!' was featured weekly in *The Halifax News For Ladies*.

Shortly after meeting Elias and Angus Junior, Rita left an envelope at the front desk of the Boscawen Inn with the explicit instructions that it be priority mailed to *The Halifax News For Ladies* in time for the morning edition. The Wentzell sisters stuck it in a desk drawer, where it remained for 100 years.

Here, for the first time in print, is that column:

AHOY, DARLINGS! By Rita MacMurphy

Ahoy, darlings! Charmed, I'm sure. Rita MacMurphy here, your fabulous and talented guide to Nova Scotia's swankiest speakeasies and most glamorous galas. I have tales from two positively hair-raising wing-dings to regale you with this week!

It's common knowledge that hobnobbing and mingling are my two great joys, but only my keenest fans and creditors know that gambling is where my true passion lies. Whether I'm sipping dark and stormies at a baccarat table or waving a fistful of cash at a back alley crab fight, games of chance give me a rush that is simply divine.

This week, my career as a gambler reached its absolute zenith, darlings, when I was invited to play in the Digby Ferry Cribbage Marathon—the most exclusive high-stakes card game in all the Maritimes!

For my darling but simple readers who are unfamiliar with the Atlantic gaming community, here's the scoop on the DFCM.

Once a month, the highest rollers in Nova Scotia, and what passes for a high roller in New Brunswick, rent a private room on the Digby ferry. As they cross the Bay of Fundy, they deal high-stakes cribbage for one hundred dollars a point, double for skunks. And last month, your fabulous narrator was the first woman to ever join their ranks. Some stuffy old crones may have won us gals the vote (snooze!) but I've kicked open the door for us to win big at ferry boat gambling (hachi machi!).

As the Queen of Nova Scotia nightlife, I feel at home at any party, speakeasy or dancery. But even I was a little star-struck by the Maritime business magnates I found myself rubbing elbows with—Alexander Keith III, Greco H. Pizza and Reginald Vogue Optical, just to name a few!

There was, however, one notable dud in the bunch: the mayor of some rinky-dink bootlegging town called Lockeport. All night long, the boorish oaf was either complaining that no one respected his awful town, or bragging about his two-bit criminal exploits. I only associate with gangsters who can croon and mayors of Truro-sized towns at minimum, so I certainly wasn't impressed.

When the fiend had the unbridled gall to criticize my radio show for a lack of guests from Lockeport, I simply snapped. I put all the money I had on the table, and challenged him to do the same. One final game—winner takes all, loser shuts their beastly mouth for the remainder of the evening.

He took the bait, and hand after hand, kitty after kitty, I played the best cribbage of my life and positively skunked the ruddy-faced vulgarian.

"Looks like Lockeport's outta luckport!" I quipped, and took possession of my winnings.

My esteemed colleagues all laughed and there was nothing 'His Honour' could do but sit there and take it.

As tends to happen, things got unfortunate once New Brunswick became involved. As the ferry entered the Port of Saint John, it gave a ghastly lurch forward, causing my fabulous new hat to fall off. A few jacks and fives may have tumbled out onto the table. But, darlings, I swear on a stack of my own headshots I haven't the foggiest notion of how they got there.

The mayor began making all sorts of simply awful allegations. But he hadn't made any friends that night and I'm a fabulous and universally beloved debutante, so I was given the benefit of the doubt.

The mayor vowed revenge, but that seemed like an impotent threat, darlings. So as anyone would, I simply took the train home, spent his money on hats, and forgot that he ever existed.

A few days later, despite my profane protestations to my producers, I was assigned to cover the *Bluenose*'s ho-hum homecoming. I have lost a small fortune betting on that good-for-nothing heap of wood and canvas. She may have won the Fisherman's Cup, but she didn't beat the spread!

The ship of ghouls was scheduled to arrive at some ungodly early hour, so I was forced to spend a night in Lunenburg. Which is truly a tragedy, because I had to miss a very prestigious Charleston dancing contest on the wings of a biplane flying over Dartmouth. (I later heard that everyone involved has died, but if I'd been there I'm quite sure it would've gone differently.)

Getting to the far-flung boat-hole was simply dreadful and it was nearly one in the morning before we arrived. A lesser woman might have called it a night, but I'd just gotten my cocaine prescription refilled and one of the side effects is trouble sleeping.

After leaving my bags with the haggard young sisters at the front desk, I hit the streets looking for action and happened upon a little speakeasy called The Knot. The atmosphere and decor did not meet my standard, but I plunked my board and pegs down on the bar, and before long I was in my element—fleecing rubes at cribbage.

I was ready to retire at the dawn's early light, when my little cribbage cadre was joined by a heavily armed bootlegger, claiming to be in the employ of 'the mayor of Lockeport'.

My radio appearance in Lunenburg had been covered in all the South Shore papers, and one of the mayor's literate advisors must have tipped him off.

The brute positively blew a gasket asking me for the Mayor's money. "Pay up or I'll cut off your this" and "You'll die a slow that" sort of thing. Frightfully rude and needlessly vulgar.

I offered to go get my chequebook, but the paranoid wretch insisted on escorting me.

Thankfully, by now it was my call time and my radio team was searching for me. Sensibly, the only bar in town was the first place they looked.

Not wanting to murder me in front of so many witnesses (from the big city, no less, therefore extra credible), he hesitated as I was hustled to the waterfront. As my listeners know, I then recorded a fantastic episode of Kitchen Party, which included witty banter and approximately an hour of singing. Let no one say I am not a professional!

After the show, I bee-lined for the train station, but found that every ticket to Halifax had already been sold to the rowdy crowd of *Bluenose* revellers.

After spotting my armed assailant skulking about, I returned to the hotel, left my mark on the drapery and then holed up in my room to await my fate.

The incident had shaken me to my core. I nearly entertained the notion that my actions could have consequences! But then, right on cue, as if angels from the Lord, the two biggest suckers I've ever seen walked through my door and offered me access to the *Bluenose*, a boat of incalculable monetary value!

I swallowed my pride and telephoned the mayor. He enthusiastically told me that the *Bluenose* would be a most satisfactory repayment. Apparently the people of Lockeport feel very looked-down-upon by Lunenburg and he saw this as a great opportunity for vengeance, or something. I don't concern myself with the motives of rural Nova Scotians.

All that remains is to actually relieve these naïve youngsters of their innocence and property. Will I pull it off yet again? Of course I shall.

Sorry to leave you on such a cliffhanger, darling readers, but duty calls! Until next time, ha cha cha and away we go!

16: An escalating tug problem

These days, FM radio is just background noise. There's an AC/DC station for Dad, a Josh Groban station for Mom and a Beyoncé station for everyone in between. That's pretty much it.

But in the early 1920s, radio was a technological marvel. Only a few years prior, if you wanted to hear a new song, you had to buy the sheet music, take piano lessons, and then play it yourself. Now, all you had to do was turn a knob on a box full of tubes and you could hear music from all over the world.

At the dawn of mass media, getting one of your songs on the radio was the equivalent of going viral on TikTok today. No one really understood how it worked or what it meant, but it seemed very important to young artists.

In their naïve excitement, Angus Junior and Elias hadn't thought to ask Rita any technical questions. Questions like, "Don't you need more than one technician to set up and produce a live nationwide broadcast from a fishing schooner?" or "Since no one can see you, why not just pretend to be on the *Bluenose* and broadcast from anywhere?" There were no satisfying answers, because this was all a scam.

Rita MacMurphy had never intended to feature Jigtallica on a real episode of her show. The only thing Mugsy's radio antenna had been broadcasting was the *Bluenose*'s location, The only person picking up the frequency was the mayor of Lockeport. The purpose of Jigtallica's music was to cover up the sound of the mayor's approaching tugboat.

Now that the band had broken up, that job fell to Rita. Although her audience had dispersed throughout the ship, she kept on singing at the top of her lungs.

Angus Junior sat on the gunwale on the *Bluenose's* starboard bow while Gwen inspected a bruise on his face. He was determined not to cry in front of her for the rest of the voyage, but he really had his work cut out for him.

"You need to work on your ground game," Gwen told him. "From watching my brothers, I would estimate 80% of fights end up on the floor."

Angus Junior winced as she touched the bruise.

"But," she continued, "this is a rare instance in which the intent is more valuable than the outcome. I'm happy you stood up for yourself."

"Thanks. I always suspected that Elias would be the first guy I'd ever punch," Angus Junior replied. "But I'll miss having friends."

"You don't need friends like that," she said, gesturing to the stern, where Elias, Rick and the Wentzells were smoking cigarettes.

Maybe Gwen was right. Maybe life after Jigtallica wouldn't be as lonely as Elias had led him to believe.

Rita began singing a traditional Irish ballad about a girl who was executed for blowing up a post office. But if you ignored the lyrics, the tune had a Sixpence None The Richer sort of vibe.

A break in the fog let in a beam of moonlight, casting Gwen in a shimmering glow.

Angus Junior was still bursting with adrenaline from the fist fight. If anything was ever going to happen between these two, the time was now. "Would you, uh, maybe want to dance with me?" he asked.

Gwen nodded as she put her arms around Angus Junior, and

they awkwardly circled around at arm's length for a while.

Elias bitterly watched them slowdance from the other side of the ship. "What a loser," he commented. "I was gonna kick him out of the band anyway."

"Elias, you're being a Grade A sook right now," said Florence.

"Rick, talk some sense into him!" Winifred added.

"Elias, me son, you're a fishing boat deserter, a kidnapper and teenager experiencing homelessness," Rick said. "Don't add 'fella with no friends' to that list. Go make up with Angus Junior and let's go home."

"I got plenty of friends. I got you guys." Elias argued.

"Not if you don't apologize to Angus Junior!" Florence told him.

"Yeah, and learn his song," Winifred added. "I wanna hear it!"

"It's not his song," Elias said, clutching his bottle of lyrics and music. "It's Jigtallica's song. And as I'm legal owner of this bottle, that means it's now my song."

Rick snatched the bottle from him. "As Jigtallica's manager, I'm taking these until this is settled," he said. "It's for your own good."

Elias grabbed for the bottle, but Rick held it above his head. Elias jumped up and tried to grab it a few times. But, as he'd learned earlier that day, a game of keep-away has no winners.

"Ugh! Some friends you are!" he pouted as he stormed off, "I'm going below deck until this stupid voyage is over. You guys all suck!"

"We suck?" Winifred called after him. "You're the one running off to hang out with the principal!"

"Yeah! Plus Angus Junior over here is about to get friggin' laid!" Florence added. "He's the cool Jigtallica member."

As Elias stomped past Angus Junior and Gwen, they barely noticed him. They were off in their own little world, and frenching was back on the agenda.

But as soon as Rita finished her song, Gwen abruptly pulled

away. "Do you hear that?"

"Uh, maybe it's my heart beating really loud," Angus Junior said, "because of, you know, my uh, feelings."

"You are breathing very loudly, but no. The sound I'm describing is a boat engine," she said, pointing out to sea. "It's coming from there."

Rita started loudly singing another song, this time about a woman who had a hard time breaking up with a leprechaun. But, no matter how loud she got, she could no longer cover up the low rumbling sound that was gradually getting louder.

Through the fog, a tugboat with a bright spotlight was barrelling toward them.

"They can help us back to shore," Gwen said. "We need to get their attention!"

"Could we maybe kiss first?" asked Angus Junior, "before the moment passes?"

"It has passed," said Gwen. "Hey! Hey! Over here!"

She waved her arms in the air to catch the boat's attention.

Rick scrambled across the ship and approached her. "Quit yer waving, sweetheart. That tug's full of thugs and they ain't to be trifled with," he yelled. "We has to drop sail and bail!"

Gwen looked out at the tugboat. It was heading straight for them and not slowing down. "Maybe you're right," she said. "Angus Junior, hoist the mainsail!"

Mugsy pointed his machine gun at Angus Junior. "Nobody's hoisting nothing, see?" he said. "Hands where I can see 'em, all of youse. Stand in a line, see?"

Everyone put their hands in the air and backed up against the gunwale as Mugsy covered them with his machine gun. "We're all just gonna float here, see? Real quiet like," he said.

"And that's been our show, darlings," said Rita. "No encores tonight, I'm afraid."

"I had a hunch that buddy with the gun was shady," Florence told her sister. "Think his tugboat's a drug boat?"

"Hey, Bedford, buddy!" Winifred shouted. "Do your tug pals know where to get some laudanum?"

"He ain't from Bedford," Rick said.

"Cram it!" Mugsy yelled.

The tugboat pulled up alongside the *Bluenose* and shut off its engine. From its deck, a red-faced man in a rumpled suit shouted through a big tin cone, the loudest amplifier available at the time.

"Attention Lunenburg scum!" he yelled. "This is the mayor of Lockeport. Prepare to be boarded!"

He threw one end of a rope onto the *Bluenose*'s deck. Mugsy handed it to Angus Junior. "You! Hitch this to the cleat, see?"

"Uh…" said Angus Junior.

Gwen did it for him.

With the tugboat lashed to the *Bluenose*, the mayor climbed aboard and slapped Mugsy on the back. "Mugsy, you've really outdone yourself this time. You're one of our town's finest criminals," he said. "I'll see you get the Order of Lockeport for this."

Everyone watched as the mayor strutted across the *Bluenose* to the helm and put his hands on the ship's wheel. Lunenburg's pride and joy was now under Lockeport's control.

Rick looked away. As he did, he caught sight of Tony, a bespectacled young man barely older than Elias. He climbed onto the *Bluenose*, holding a clipboard.

"Great work, Mr. Mayor," Tony said. "The base is really going to eat this up. Now, let me just do a quick head count on these prisoners here. One, two…Wait, Rick? What are you doing here?"

"Tony?" Rick asked. "You're working for the friggin' mayor? After what he done? After what I done?!"

Rick was a lifelong stoic. He didn't even cry the day his parents both went out for cigarettes and neither one ever came back. But in that moment he could not look Tony in the eye without shedding a tear.

"Wow, it really is you," said the mayor. "Don't cry, there, Ricky boy. You ought to be happy Tony got himself a job with the municipality. That's more than you ever had."

"Rick," Angus Junior asked, "how do you know so many people from Lockeport?"

"Because," Rick answered after a deep breath, "I'm *from* Lockeport."

Everyone gasped. If you were from Lunenburg and one of your good friends revealed that, you'd gasp, too. It would be a big-enough cliffhanger to end a book chapter on.

17: Elias' last-ditch effort

As the marauding Lockeporters took control of the *Bluenose*, Elias was below deck. He sat on the edge of a bunk with his head in his hands, unable to hear the commotion above over the sounds of his own sulking.

"My dad's funeral was last night, you know?" he bemoaned. "I'm not saying I should get a whole weekend to get over it or anything, but I do wish people would cut me a little slack!"

Hennigar, still gagged and tied to the bunk beside him, struggled to break free. He'd spent some time in his early 20s at a forced-labour camp in occupied Belgium, so he actually found being forcibly restrained kind of nostalgic. But listening to a vulnerable teenager open up about his feelings was more than he could endure. It went against everything he stood for.

"You know what else?" Elias continued. "I've actually been feeling sad about my body lately, too. It's just been changing so fast."

Hennigar shouted muffled curses to try and drown out the emotional outburst.

"Enough with the yammerin', see?" said Mugsy, as he climbed below deck. "Come on up and join the party."

"Oh, hey, Mugsy, what are you sayin'?" Elias said. "Did Angus Junior send you down here to apologize? Well, he can tell me himself! Actually, while you're down here, I'd love to pick your brain about the radio business."

"Wise up, kid! There ain't no radio show, see?" Mugsy said. "It was all just a flim flam to take the *Bluenose*, see? And you fell for it, hook, line and sinker."

He pointed his Tommy gun at Elias. "Now, get your no good keester upstairs!"

Something inside Elias snapped. He had never been outschemed before. He hadn't even considered it a possibility.

He hopped off the bunk and got in Mugsy's face. "Is Rita Mac-Murphy even a real singer?" he shouted, "or is everything a lie?!"

"I've got something true for you right here, see?" Mugsy said, as he pushed the gun barrel into Elias' chest. "I'm gonna pump you full of lead if you're not upstairs on the count of three!"

As Mugsy started to count, the *Bluenose* suddenly lurched. She had been tied to the Lockeporters' tugboat, and when the tugging started the whole ship was yanked forward. The sudden jostling knocked Mugsy's sea legs out from under him. He fell backward to the ground, dropping his gun.

Elias did not hesitate to scrap.

Meanwhile, up above, Rita MacMurphy was getting bored. Now that the singing and deception were over, she had nothing to do but hang around with a bunch of small-timers like the mayor of Lockeport.

"You'll have to do a concert in Lockeport sometime Miss MacMurphy," the mayor said. "I run a little speakeasy on the side, we get all kinds of bands through there. In fact, I haven't booked anyone for my inaugural ball yet—"

"You couldn't afford me, darling," Rita said. "I believe my debt has been paid for our little misunderstanding on the ferry, yes?"

"We're absolutely square, ma'am. This is about something more important than money. It's about civic pride. Once I tug this tub back to Lockeport, we'll have settled the score with Lunenburg once and for all."

"So we're actually going to Lockeport? What time is the next train out of town, darling?"

"Lockeport doesn't have a train station. Someone can drive you to the one in Shelburne tomorrow morning," the mayor responded.

"This deal is getting worse all the time!" Rita fumed.

She looked over at the Lunenburgers, still lined up at the gunwale. Tony had a gun trained on them.

Rita walked up behind him and put her hand gently on his shoulder. "While we're all just floating around, be a dear and search them for me, would you?" she said. "I believe they have contraband."

Tony looked to the mayor, who nodded with approval.

"Those two first, if you don't mind," Rita said, pointing at the Wentzell sisters.

Tony walked over and started patting Florence down.

"Hands off!" she yelled. "I don't like getting groped by guys who wear glasses!"

Tony found a flask of rum in her garter. "I'll hold on to that, thank you, darling," Rita said, "as well as any other bottles you may find."

Winifred and Florence silently vowed revenge as Tony took all of their concealed bottles and handed them to Rita.

"Sorry, old sports. Spoils of war and all that," she said, after taking a long nip. "I simply cannot be expected to spend a night in Lockeport and remember it."

Tony couldn't look Rick in the eye as he frisked him.

"Does your ma know this is what you're doing?" Rick asked.

Tony didn't answer. He took Elias' bottle from around Rick's neck and tossed it to Rita.

"Do I look like I drink paper?" she responded. "Use some sense, darling."

She opened the bottle and looked at some of the Jigtallica lyrics inside. "'*Sad Halibut True*'?" she read in disgust. "What is this tripe?"

Before she could throw the lyrics bottle away, Mugsy climbed up on deck. He had his hands in the air, as Elias climbed up right behind him, poking Hennigar's bayonet into his back.

"Listen up, whoever you are!" Elias yelled. "I took an intensive throat-cutting course today, and I'm ready to put it into practice!"

The mayor seemed very much in his element as he pointed a handgun at Elias. Clearly, this wasn't his first standoff. "Look, kid, this is Lockeport municipal politics. You can't win here," he said. "Put the gun down."

"I knew Elias would save us!" Angus Junior whispered to Gwen.

"I remain skeptical," she whispered back.

"Ang-Ju, buddy!" Elias shouted, "the radio show wasn't real! No one heard us break up, so it's like it never even happened. We can totally get a do over!"

"Uh…" Angus Junior responded. "That's not really my priority."

The mayor inched closer. "Just drop it, kid," he urged.

Elias pushed Mugsy out of his way and pointed the rifle straight at the mayor. "You're wearing a big sash that says Mayor, so I assume you're in charge. Tell your men to steer this boat to the nearest radio station. Miss MacMurphy, you're going to introduce me on the radio tonight and I don't care how!"

"This is more in line with my expectations," Gwen whispered to Angus Junior.

"From now on, you guys are either with me or against me!" Elias shouted at his friends. "If you're not going to help me get on the radio, then you can get in a dory and row yourselves home, for all I care!"

"Your sound is simply too raw, darling," Rita said as she lit a cigarette. "I will not be associated with that kind of noise. If you wanted to be a real musician, you should've run away and joined the vaudeville circuit as a child."

Elias' eyes went wide as Rita held up the bottle full of his lyrics and uncorked it. She dipped her lit cigarette inside, and the bottle started filling with smoke.

"Now, I must insist that you drop the gun and don't ever tell me my business again, or I swear to God I'll burn this drivel right here and now," she said.

As the heat of the cigarette threatened the lyrics to *Angler of Death*, Elias felt a sharp pain, as though Rita were burning his own flesh. "Okay, you win!" he yelled, and lowered the rifle.

As Rita pulled the cigarette out of the bottle, Mugsy grabbed the rifle from Elias and smacked him across the mouth with it.

"That's for making me look bad in front of the mayor, see?" he grumbled. "Now, get over there with the rest of the Lunenburg losers. Shmaa!"

"Can I have my lyrics back, at least?" Elias asked.

"Not a chance, darling," Rita said, tucking the bottle into her purse. "When I get back to the city, my friends and I are going to read these aloud and make fun of them. It'll be a scream!"

Elias slunk over to his friends. "Hey guys. What are you sayin'? Sorry about the 'with me or against me' thing. I misspoke there. But I think we can agree that the Lockeport guys are the ones who are really in the wrong here, right? They are from Lockeport, after all."

No one answered.

18: So here's the deal with Lockeport

Maybe other parts of the world have more nuance, but on Nova Scotia's South Shore, some towns are good and some towns are evil. Some evil towns accept it, like Bridgewater. If you go there, something bad is going to happen to you. That's just how it is.

Other evil towns, like Lockeport, have a real chip on their shoulder about it. It's not their fault they're evil. If such and such misfortune hadn't befallen them, things would be different.

These are the towns you have to watch out for.

Years before the night of our story, a committee of Nova Scotian investors began planning to build a racing schooner to compete in the Fisherman's Cup. Lunenburg was the obvious choice for where to build, but since the committee was relying on government grant funding, they technically had to do interviews with every shipyard that applied. It was in that spirit that the Bluenose Building Committee made the pity trip to the Township of Lockeport.

There, the newly-elected mayor had just run a two-pronged election strategy. First, he had used his criminal connections to bribe and intimidate all the right people. Second, he had made a lot of grandiose promises about restoring Lockeport's supposedly-lost honour. Having a prestigious racing boat under Lockeport's control would help his popularity with voters and racketeers alike.

To impress the *Bluenose* committee, The Mayor commissioned a statue of a ship's wheel to be unveiled during their visit. Where else in Nova Scotia could you see something like that, after all?

A lot was riding on this statue, but no one in Lockeport was confident enough in their literacy to come up with a good inscription. And not having a library nearby, no one was able to look up "Inspiring statue quotes". The day before the committee arrived, the task was given to the high-school student with the best marks in English class. His only instructions were to write something nautical-sounding.

A huge crowd gathered to greet the committee, and patiently stood through a bunch of speeches by local 'dignitaries' about how visiting Lockeport is totally worth the long drive.

When the mayor finally pulled the tarp off the statue, the inscription read:

ERECTED FOR THE SEAMEN

First, only one teen chuckled. Then another, and another. Before long, the snickering had built to a cacophony of laughter that could be heard from as far away as Digby. Shouts of "Oh, grow up!" and "Real mature!" did little to stop Lockeport from becoming the laughingstock of Shelburne County that day.

Stifling a giggle, the committee chairman told the mayor that the decision was not yet final but Lockeport was a real 'up and comer'. Then the whole committee laughed in the mayor's face. They bid farewell, and construction of the *Bluenose* began in Lunenburg soon after.

At the moment of the statue's unveiling, Rick was in the bedroom of the widow Constance Lohnes. He leaned back in a rocking chair, biting into a ripe orange and letting the juice fall down his chin, and watched her brush her hair. The townspeople's raucous laughter inflamed their passions and they made love for the second time that afternoon.

Neither of them knew it would be their last.

When Constance's son Tony came home that afternoon, he ran upstairs and immediately shut his bedroom door, loudly cursing to himself.

The jaded professional Rick of 1922 would know better than to get involved. But, much like the pornography stars of today, the Rick of 1919 was just a wide-eyed 18-year-old boy in love with an older mommy figure.

"I'll go talk to him, man to man," he said, putting on some cutoffs made out of long underwear.

He knocked on Tony's door and got no reply. But like anyone from Nova Scotia, this did not deter him. He opened the door and found Tony erasing a chalkboard full of permutations on the phrase "Erected for seamen."

"I just thought it would be funny, Rick," Tony pleaded. "I didn't think they'd actually use it!"

There was a heavy knock at the front door. Tony's face went white.

"Just a moment!" Constance called from her room.

Rick had no idea what was going on. But as he watched Constance walk downstairs, he knew he would do anything to protect her.

"Tony, me son," he said. "Whatever the fuss, we'll sort 'er out as teen father and teen son. Now, tell me what happened."

Constance answered the front door. The mayor stood on the porch. Behind him was an angry rabble of villagers wielding torches and harpoons.

In the immediate aftermath of the town-wide humiliation, angry and confused Lockeporters were looking for someone to blame. The mayor had sprung into action and led the mob straight to the house of the no-good punk who had written the inscription.

"Step aside, ma'am," he said. "We have reason to believe your son is a traitor to Lockeport."

"My Tony? But he's such a nice young man. He would never!" she answered, clutching her bathrobe.

"Step aside, ma'am or we'll burn the house down," said the mayor. "Won't we, boys?"

The crowd roared. The mayor had been wondering how far he could take Lockeport down the road to mob rule, and now he knew: Pretty far.

"Wait a minute now!" Rick yelled from the top of the stairs.

He walked down to the mayor, with Tony sheepishly following behind him.

"Listen, me b'ys. It's a sin what happened today," Rick told them. "But I tell you, Tony is some innocent and I'm right guilty."

"Rick, what's happening?" asked Constance.

"Tony don't even know what those weenus and jism words mean. He's just a boy of 16. But me, I'm a little older than that. I'm the one responsible," Rick continued. "I made Tony write the semen thing. Told him I'd beat him up if he didn't put that on there."

"Tony, is this true?" Constance asked.

Rick knew what his fellow Lockeporters were capable of. He'd been good at comforting Constance after the loss of her husband, but he could never truly comfort her if she lost her son. He took a deep breath and did what he had to do. "It's true as a trawler!" he yelled. "I'm just a jokester. I don't care nothin' for Lockeport or anyone livin' here! Tell 'em, Tony!"

"I'm sorry everyone!" Tony said. "Rick made me do it. I didn't even know what he was telling me to write!"

"That's all the evidence I need!" yelled the mayor. "Rick, you are hereby banished from Lockeport and the surrounding catchment area!"

Constance didn't even try to stop the angry mob from pulling Rick out of the house. "How could I have let you into my home?" she wept. "You've ruined our town and corrupted my Tony!"

That afternoon, Rick was placed in a dory with nothing but a jar of chow chow for sustenance and launched out to sea. He rowed his way up the South Shore, leaving a string of satisfied widows from Hunt's Point to Lunenburg. But he never truly loved again.

He had always hoped that it had been worth it, that maybe Tony had taken his comedy gifts and gone pro, or even done something of value to the world. But that night on the *Bluenose*, he finally had to let that dream die.

19: The Big Shove-Off

Captain Angus Walters first went to sea as an eight-year-old throater and worked his way up to captain of his own ship. He had commanded that ship through two fishing seasons in the Grand Banks and sailed her into the history books with back to back Fisherman's Cup wins. The *Bluenose* had given everyone in Lunenburg something to feel superior about forevermore.

Then his son selfishly took it all away and handed it over to pirates from Lockeport.

Angus Junior knew he had also destroyed the lives of all his friends. After their role in the loss of the *Bluenose*, they'd all be shunned from Lunenburg society. Every party in town would be planned behind the Wentzell sisters' backs. No widow would ever give Rick a friendly tug behind the Scotia Trawler again, let alone invite him to stay in their home.

Angus Junior couldn't really relate to Elias' pain over losing his dream, because he had never really had a dream himself. But he still felt bad. If he had just told Elias the truth about the radio show that morning, none of this would have happened.

He had led Gwen the furthest astray. Few navigators ever come back from a 0-1 record for losing boats.

Angus Junior knelt on the deck of the *Bluenose,* with his back against the starboard gunwale. Gwen, Elias, Rick and the Wentzells all knelt in a line beside him, under the barrel of the mayor of Lockeport's Tommy gun. Rita MacMurphy was sort of pointing a gun at them, too, but she was mostly twirling it around and pointing it at seagulls. She was pretty buzzed by this point.

A good politician knows the importance of one-on-one connection, so the mayor took a moment to point his gun in each person's face individually.

When he got to Gwen, Angus Junior thought about touching her hand to comfort her. But he didn't want to make her feel pressured into holding hands on top of everything else.

"Uh...hey!" he mumbled at the mayor. "Do whatever you want to my dad's boat, just don't hurt my friends!"

"Don't be a sook, kid. We're not here to kill anybody, we're just here to right a wrong," said the mayor. "The *Bluenose* should've been built in Lockeport! We were robbed and now we're just robbing you back."

"Lockeport? Build this boat?" Florence scoffed. "You must be out of your Jesus mind!"

"Only race a Lockeport boat could win is one to the bottom of the ocean, am I right?" Winifred added.

Florence and Winifred high-fived each other.

"Kids like you cost our town everything," the mayor yelled, "with your smart-mouth comments about our statue!"

"Oh, right! I remember hearing about a funny statue in some town out by Shelburne," Florence said. "Forgot it was Lockeport."

"What's it say again?" Winifred asked. "And Peeners For All, or something?"

"Erected for the Semen, it says," Rick said, looking at the mayor.

All the Lunenburgers laughed at that, even Gwen.

"Stop that! It's not funny!" the mayor yelled. "After we lost the *Bluenose* contract, our town had no choice but to transition to a petty crime economy."

"I coulda been somebody!" Mugsy cried as he tied a rope to a cleat.

"Uh…I don't see how any of this means *Bluenose* was stolen from you guys, *per se*," Angus Junior said.

"It's tremendously unlikely that a statue inscription was a factor in where a ship was built," Gwen said.

"I said shut up!" yelled the mayor. "Our town lost everything because of the statue inscription, not because of any of my policies, end of story!"

Mugsy and Tony approached the mayor.

"Lifeboat secure, sir," Tony told him, and gestured to a dory drifting in the water, tied to the *Bluenose*.

The mayor smiled. "Get off my ship," he told the Lunenburgers, in a tough-guy tone that he had clearly rehearsed.

"This is friggin' trash," Florence shouted. "It's not our town's fault you guys have a dumb statue and we have the world's fastest boat!"

"Florence, me girl," Rick cautioned, "don't play games wit' him. You ain't know what the mayor of Lockeport is capable of."

He slowly stood up. Under the mayor's watchful eye, he climbed over the *Bluenose*'s gunwale and gingerly lowered himself into the dory below.

"Now the rest of ya, see?" Mugsy yelled, firing his gun in the air.

"Fine, whatever!" Florence scoffed, getting up and dusting herself off."

"This party's dead anyways," Winifred added.

"Heh, heh, heh, erected," Florence laughed.

"Heh, heh, heh, semen," Winifred giggled.

Everyone laughed at the statue inscription again as Rick helped the Wentzells into the dory. Tense as the situation was, no one could deny that it was pretty funny.

Elias got up next. No one needed to point a gun at him. Instead, Rita pointed hers at the bottle of lyrics.

"Off the boat darling, or I'll incinerate this mediocrity," she said.

"I feel personally insulted that you considered these worthy of my valuable time."

Elias thought about explaining that his songs were actually ahead of their time, and that a trend-chasing sellout like her just didn't get them, but instead he climbed overboard as ordered.

"Hey, uh, it's gonna be okay," Angus Junior told Gwen.

"What? Where do you see evidence of that?" she asked.

He tried to summon his inner Elias and convince her that he had a plan. "Uh, so, if you navigate us all home in the dory, I'll sign a confession saying it was all my fault and I forced you to come with me. I'll make a run for it and be in Bridgewater by morning, where I'll disappear into the crowded slums."

Gwen looked down at the dory, full of reprobates, bobbing on the choppy sea, then back at Angus Junior. All of the complex variables had collapsed into a simple choice. Did she trust him, yes or no?

She took a deep breath and climbed over the gunwale.

"I'm, uh, right behind you," Angus Junior assured her as Rick helped her into the dory. "Maybe in a few years, when the heat dies down, you can don a disguise and come find me in the Bridgewater underground. If you want, I mean. No pressure or anything."

After Gwen made it safely into the dory, the mayor grabbed Angus Junior by the scruff of the neck. "You're staying with us, kid," he said. "You're our insurance policy. If your dad ever wants to see you alive, he'll sign the *Bluenose* over to us, nice and legal."

Angus Junior wasn't sure his father would make that trade. He struggled with all his might, but the mayor overpowered him.

Gwen could only watch. As one of five people crammed into a small boat for two, any sudden movements she made could tip the whole thing over.

"Quit squirming, kid!" the mayor ordered. "Mugsy, calm him down. Tony, cut them loose."

Mugsy took a small bottle of laudanum out of his pocket and poured some onto a rag. Angus Junior was already hyperventilating when Mugsy held the anaesthetic up to his face.

"Shh, see?" he said. "Sniff up this snootful of sleepy sauce."

Meanwhile, Tony picked up Hennigar's bayonet and held it to the rope that hitched the dory to the *Bluenose*.

"I'm sorry, this isn't personal," he said, slicing the rope. "It's just municipal politics."

The tether between Angus Junior and his only friends had been severed. He faintly heard Gwen's voice on the wind, calling out for him. Then he fell into a deep, laudanum-induced sleep.

"Heist well done, boys," said the mayor, letting Angus Junior fall flat on the deck. "After tonight, Lockeport will be the most important town on the South Shore, and Lunenburg will be nothing but an afterthought. The way it should be!"

The mayor and his lackeys' delusional laughter filled the night sky as the dory drifted away.

"Aw, nuts!" Mugsy exclaimed after a moment. "We got one more guy tied up downstairs. I forgot to put him in the dory."

"Well, if he's already tied up, we may as well take him with us," the mayor responded. "No harm, no foul."

"No harm, no foul," Rita repeated in a mocking tone. "Sloppy process ends in sloppy results, darlings, and you three are perfectly sloppy. Some big bad wolves you are, way out in Lockeport. You flops wouldn't last a week in the North End."

"Why don't you have another drink, Miss MacMurphy?" the mayor said.

"Why don't I, indeed?" Rita muttered, taking another gulp from the Wentzells' bottle. "You're all a bunch of flops!"

After a pause, the mayor tried to start up the evil laughter again, but Rita had made them all feel self-conscious about it.

The moment was ruined.

20: Never-ending dory

Put the client first, don't get involved with the family, make sure your hair smells nice. Widow-comforters who uphold these core tenets have always found success on Nova Scotia's South Shore, while grave misfortunes have befallen those who disobey.

Twice in his life, Rick had broken these rules, and both times he found himself adrift in the Atlantic. The first time had been a crime of passion. When he took the heat for Tony, he did it to protect the love of his life. Up until that night, he had always believed it was worth it.

But this time, he should have known better. He'd abandoned his client, let her son talk him into crime after crime, and left his jar of good-smelling hair cream shattered on the sidewalk. And for what?

Rick pondered his changing attitude toward his past and present surrogate sons as everyone bobbed up and down in a dory and watched the *Bluenose* vanish into the fog. They had agreed that they'd start rowing to shore in a minute; they just needed to float for a bit and have a quick smoke first.

"Cannot believe that friggin' guy had laudanum on him the whole time," Winifred grumbled, lighting a cigarette.

"Friggin' Lockeport, eh?" Florence groused. "Rick, how could you even be from there?"

"Sorry, me ol' trouts, this here's all my fault," he said with a sigh. "I broke the rules, and now we's all paying for it."

Elias held out two fingers in front of Rick. As he always did, Rick took a cigarette out of his pack and handed it to him. Elias took a drag without a thankful word or even a gracious nod.

"I never should've let any of this happen," Rick said, as much to himself as anyone else.

"Rick, don't misallocate your mental resources by blaming yourself," Gwen assured him. "Clearly, this is Elias' fault!"

"What?" Elias asked. "How is this my fault?"

It was too foggy to see everyone's skeptical looks, but Elias could feel them. He got defensive. "None of this was my idea! Angus Junior was the one who told Rita we'd steal the *Bluenose*. I was just executing on his vision, like I do in the band."

Gwen knew she should prioritize the harmony of the rowing crew over her own anger. But, as she had feared, her feelings for Angus Junior influenced her decision-making. She was not going to let Elias get away with this one.

"You execute Angus Junior's vision?" she said. "Pardon my strong language, but that's a dubious claim! You've never prioritized his vision. You couldn't even remember the lyrics to his song."

"Well, maybe if he spent more time rehearsing with me and less time with you, no one would've forgotten anything," Elias answered.

"You're presenting a false binary. If you had wanted to learn the song, you would've," Gwen responded. "I've been observing the two of you for months, and in nearly all cases, you do whatever you want."

"Everything I do, I do for Jigtallica," Elias responded. "And until you started sniffing around, turning him against me, Jigtallica meant both me and Ang-Ju!"

"You listen to what Angus Junior has to say less than 15% of the time, while your demands on him have grown exponentially," Gwen said. "The data suggests that your own actions turned him against you."

"No one asked for your data, Gwen. No one asked you for any-thing," Elias scoffed. "You were there, Rick. Back me up on this! Stealing the *Bluenose* was Ang-Ju's idea, right?"

Rick was slow to answer. "I suppose Angus Junior was the first one of you fellers to bring up stealing the *Bluenose*, but—"

"But what?" Elias snapped. "Are you gonna try and pin all this on me, too? No loyalty when the chips are down, just like a Locke-porter!"

"Elias!" Winifred gasped. "Just because he's from Lockeport don't mean you gotta call him that."

"You're coming at me too, Win? What is wrong with you people?" Elias shouted. "You think I don't feel bad enough without all of you ganging up on me?"

"Ah, here he goes," Florence muttered. "Winnie, I told you we shouldn't party with Elias. He's right uptight, and the night always ends with him having a conniption. Just cause he's in a band don't mean he's fun."

"You're right, Flo," Winifred answered. "This kinda thing never happened when we used to party with Tommy Diddler."

"You know why this never happens to Tommy Diddler?" Elias asked. "Because nothing ever happens to Tommy Diddler. He doesn't have the vision to make things happen!"

He got to his feet and pointed his cigarette at Winifred. "Don't you ever compare me to Tommy Diddler! I play music that the world needs to hear, that no-talent violinist is just in it for the drink tickets."

"Elias, sit down!" Gwen yelled. "You're rocking the boat."

"I'm an artist! Rocking the boat is what I do!" Elias yelled back. "You people don't get it. I can't just sit down and do what I'm told like everyone else!"

"Lord dyin'!" yelled Florence, "you're being some dramatic, Elias! Just sit down!"

As the sea got choppier, Elias grew more and more dangerous to the vessel's balance with each passionate gesticulation. "You all want me to be just like the rest of the mindless little fish out there!" he shouted. "Working my life away on some boat, listening to mass-produced sea shanties!"

"Rick, you need to restrain him by any means necessary, as quickly as possible," Gwen said, "before he tips us over and drags us all down with him."

Rick knew she was right. He took a final drag on his cigarette, flicked it overboard, then gingerly rose to his feet. "Elias me son, if you wanna rant and rave like an arse pick tomorrow, fill yer boots. But no more tonight. Man to man, I'm giving you one last chance to sit down before I choke you right the frig out."

"Never!" Elias yelled. "I will not be silenced!"

Rick sighed. He really didn't want to do this, but he'd been left with no choice. With lightning speed, he grabbed Elias by the neck with both hands. "Shh, just take 'er easy, me son," he said. "For your own good, just take a snooze the rest of the way home."

"Rick, you can't do this to me!" Elias choked. "You're not my real dad! You're not even my fake dad!"

Rick's fingers tightened on Elias' windpipe. But as Elias started coughing, Rick became horrified at where things were heading, and let go.

Not expecting to be released so suddenly, Elias kept struggling and knocked himself backwards off the side of the dory and into the cold water.

"Elias!" Rick shouted, and reached in after him.

It was no use. Everyone shouted for Elias, until the dory rose and fell on a big wave. Then another. They all clung to the sides as their little boat was tossed around.

By the time the sea calmed down, Elias was long gone.

21: Poor unfortunate souls

Some time later, Elias awoke in what appeared to be his childhood bedroom. But as he got up and looked around, he started to notice some subtle differences. For one, his blanket was made out of seaweed, and his pillow was a sea sponge. Pastel jellyfish were painted on the walls, and a seahorse mobile hung above a driftwood crib.

The biggest difference though, was that the room was full of water instead of air. And yet, Elias could breathe.

He faintly heard an adult contemporary song coming from the other side of the door. When the chorus kicked in, he realized it was not a human singing, but a dolphin.

He followed the melodic screeches out of the bedroom and down the hallway.

In an underwater sewing room, a mermaid sat in a rocking chair made of a giant clam shell, smiling and holding her pregnant belly. She looked out the window as she listened to a conch shell record player.

But as Elias approached her, she let out an ear splitting shriek.

"What are you sayin', mer-ma'am? Sorry to surprise you. I would've said something, but I wasn't sure if I could talk down here," Elias said. "What's that music you're listening to? It's not really my kind of thing, but the vocals go some hard."

The mermaid looked Elias over, but didn't speak to him directly. "Jiminy!" she shouted. "He's awake!"

In the biggest underwater surprise yet, Elias' father walked up the stairs. "Elias, what are you speaking?"

"Oh, you know," Elias responded. "Just wondering where I am and if I'm dead, but other than that, things are fair to middling."

"Looks like you drowned," Jiminy said. "I'm your next of kin under the sea, so I guess they sent you here. I see you've met Denise."

"I'll leave you boys to catch up," said Denise the mermaid.

As she swam away, she stopped to give Elias' dad a little kiss on the cheek. "Don't forget, my parents are coming at seven."

"I thought that was tomorrow," said Jiminy.

"No. The reef guy is coming tomorrow. Dinner with my parents is tonight," she said. "And we are not cancelling on them again!"

Denise swam down the stairs, muttering to herself.

Elias and his father stood quietly for a time.

"It's not that I'm unhappy to see you," Jiminy said after a long pause. "It's just not a great time, with the baby on the way. We're not sure if it's gonna be mer or not, so that's been stressful. It's a whole thing. But we'll figure something out. So, how's school?"

"I dropped out to focus on music, remember?" Elias said.

"Oh, right. Your mom was mad about that, I think. Mandolin, right?"

"Fiddle."

"Sure, sure. Well good on you. You died doing what you loved. Like me!" Jiminy said. "Feels good, huh?"

"Not really," Elias said. "I always thought dying for your music was the coolest thing you could do. But now that I've really had the biscuit, I'm not so sure. I should've been nicer to my friends."

"Who cares? Who even needs friends?" Jiminy ranted. "They never did nothing for me. My friends, your mother, you, none of them! Everyone just stood in the way of my dream to make love to a mermaid. Then I met Denise, and as soon as she sang me her siren song, I stripped down and jumped into the water. I've never been happier. No regrets."

"Well, I hope this friggin' weird dream is worth it." Elias said, "When you jumped down here, you left me and Ma with nothing. I had to go to sea! What about *my* dream?"

"I did what I had to," his dad responded. "I couldn't live like a mindless little fish anymore. Doing the same thing on a boat every day, it was boring!"

"Jiminy!" Denise called from downstairs. "Can you help me with something in the kitchen?"

"Look, I'm sorry you and your mom needed money for rent and food," Jiminy said, "but that's society's fault, not mine."

"Jiminy!" Denise yelled. "Kitchen!"

"I heard you the first time, Denise!" Jiminy yelled back. "Look, Elias. We'll catch up later, I gotta take care of this."

Jiminy walked downstairs, leaving Elias alone.

"You can't just spring something like this on me, Jiminy!" Denise yelled. "The stress isn't good for the baby!"

"You think I asked for this?" he yelled back. "What do you want me to tell him? Huh?"

Elias sighed and slumped into the clam shell rocking chair. He looked out the window, up at the moon's reflection on the ocean's surface. He wished he could be part of that world.

As he thought about the life he had lost on land, Elias surprised himself. He didn't regret that Jigtallica would never play on the radio, or that thrash fiddle would never rise to prominence in popular culture. His deepest regret was that he'd never get to make things right with Angus Junior.

Over the years, Elias had been in bands with people all over the South Shore, but they'd all fallen apart after a rehearsal or two. Angus Junior was the only one who would ever spend all weekend jamming. He was the only one who would do shows with him every night. The only one who'd go along with his schemes, barely needing to be talked into them.

Elias had been willing to risk it all for his music, but Angus Junior had been willing to risk it all for him. Now he was in Lockeport, drugged up and alone, all because he'd put his faith in his friendship with Elias. For his sins, Elias knew that he deserved to listen to his dad and step-merm bicker for all eternity. But Angus Junior didn't deserve any of this.

He opened the window and yelled into the sea, "Ang-Ju, I'm so sorry, buddy! I treated you as a tin flutist first and a friend second. If I could do it all over again, I'd switch up the order, for sure. Ocean God, or Sea Jesus, or whoever it is down here, don't let 'er end like this. Just give me one more chance! Let me use my scheming power to get Ang-Ju home safe. Whatever happens to me after that, I don't care!"

Suddenly, a beam of white light shone through the open window and bathed Elias in its glow. A powerful current started pulling him up toward the surface.

"It's not your time, son," Jiminy said, coming back up the stairs. "But before you go, I have something for you."

He took some sand dollars out of Denise's purse. "When you get back to the surface, take this to the Bridgewater dog track. Place it all on Lucky Dan. Then take the winnings and flush them down a sewer pipe, understand? I'll be waiting."

"Sure," Elias said. "Have a good one, Dad. Have a good one forever."

Elias turned away and swam toward the surface, along the beam of celestial light, until he disappeared.

"Jiminy!" Denise yelled. "I told you not to leave your boots right in front of the door! Why do you even wear them down here? Company's coming and this place is a manatee sty!"

"Jesus, Jesus, Jesus," Elias' dad mumbled to himself. "Some friggin' dream this turned out to be."

22: Resurrected for the seamen

When Elias awoke again, he was lying flat on his back in a dory. He heard familiar voices.

"Yar! This lad's windpipe be clogged with sea water!" Polluto shouted. "He be needing a tracheotomy, the most advanced throat cut of all!"

"Wow, good idea, boss," said Petey. "Only you could pull off something like that!"

But before Polluto could attempt the delicate procedure, Elias coughed up a lungful of water into his face and started gasping for air. He leaned over the side of the dory.

When he saw the moon's reflection on the sea, he realized that he was back on the other side. He'd gotten his second chance.

"Oh, hey, Polluto, what are you sayin'?" he said. "Sorry for spitting water on you, I promise that was a survival instinct, nothing personal. And sorry for bumping into you this morning. I've heard around town that really thorns you."

"I forgive ye," Polluto said, wiping his face. "I were young once. We all caused some bumps in our days. Important thing is yer alive, and yer fingers ain't too frozen to cut fish throats. We can chalk this morning up to first day jitters, and ye can start throatin' for real at first light."

"Wow! Way to be the bigger man, boss," Petey assured him. "You're showing real growth!"

"Look, guys, I'll be honest with you. You're on my list of people to make things right with, but you're nowhere near the top," Elias told them. "So, while I appreciate you saving me, I just can't cut those throats. I've gotta get to Lockeport."

"Wow, Lockeport is a hot topic tonight, hey boss?" Petey said as he pulled on the oars. "We just picked up your pals a few minutes ago, and they all had Lockeport on the brain, too!"

"Yar, youths today! All just a bunch of Lockeport lovin' lollygaggers!" Polluto scoffed. "Except yer friend Florence...She ain't seeing anybody by any chance, is she?"

"Hmm, I'm not totally sure," Elias said, feeling bad that he had never asked the Wentzell sisters anything about themselves. "I don't think so."

"Eee!" Petey squealed. "You gotta go for it, boss!"

"Yar right!" Polluto said. "Ye really think she'd be interested?"

"Only one way to find out, boss!" Petey answered. "Eee!"

"Yar! Shut up!" Polluto yelled, turning bright red. "I think I sees the ship."

A spotlight slowly came into view through the fog.

"Ahoy!" a voice called out in the distance.

"Ahoy!" Polluto called back.

Petey rowed as hard as he could toward the spotlight. As they got close, Elias could make out the *Theresa E Creamer*, the ship he'd abandoned that morning.

"We found the ungrateful bugger!" Polluto called to the first mate, who was leaning against the *Creamer*'s gunwale.

"Great job, guys," the first mate shouted back, throwing down a rope. "There's an extra hardtack ration below deck with your names on it."

"See, skipper?" Petey shouted. "We can stay on task when we work together! You should let us be partners more often!"

As Elias climbed aboard, the first mate was less than thrilled to see his prodigal throater return.

"What are you sayin', sir?" Elias said. "Petey was sayin' that you guys picked up my friends. What are they sayin'? They sayin' everything okay?"

"Elias, I don't want to hear a word from you," the first mate said. "Do you understand how much paperwork is involved when somebody jumps overboard? It took me all morning! Now I have to do a whole other batch about dragging you and your burnout friends out of the ocean."

"Gwen's not a burnout, to be fair," Elias responded. "But, point taken."

"Just shut up and try not to die of hypothermia," The first mate said, handing him a blanket. "I've got enough to deal with without having to write a third report about you."

He stormed off below deck.

"Okay, but I need a ride out to Locke—" Elias began following him, but Rick's hand on his shoulder stopped him.

"Elias, me son, he's tired and emotional," Rick said. "You'll have better luck later if you just give him some space."

"Oh, hey, Rick," Elias said. "What are you sayin'?"

"They picked us up about fifteen minutes ago. Good thing, too, 'cause we started taking on water after you fell out," Rick said. "I been leanin' over the rail, looking at the sea for ye ever since. I would've gone out there myself, but they wouldn't lend me a dory. All their spares is full of fish. I guess they got so far behind on cutting the throats that everything's backed up."

"These guys just don't know what they're doing, eh?" Elias mused.

Rick handed Elias his nearly-empty pack of cigarettes. "Here, me old trout, you need one of these here worse than I do."

"Nah, you only got three left," Elias said. "Maybe just save me a couple drags next time you have one. Rick...About what happened on the dory. You're more of a fake dad to me than my real dad ever was. Sorry I've been such a lousy fake son."

"Elias, me son, I's sorry, too," Rick told him, deeply touched by his kind words and improved smoker's etiquette. "I should never have let go of ye so fast. I didn't mean to let ye fall in."

"That's okay," said Elias. "I learned a lot down there. Now, as Jigtallica's manager, what do you say we go get the band back together?"

Elias and Rick made their way down to the galley, where the Wentzell sisters leaned against a counter and shared some hardtack with Polluto and Petey. Gwen sat at the mess table, poring over some maps and charts with a compass.

"Hey Elias," said Winifred. "How was your trip down to drown town?"

"Glad you made it out," Florence added. "The party's just getting interesting."

"Flo, Win, I just wanna say, you were right. I did go Hali, and I'm sorry," Elias said. "I've been a bad friend all night, maybe even longer."

"There you go, being right dramatic again," Winifred told him. "You may not always be fun, but at least you ain't boring."

"Plus, we just met a couple of strapping young sailors," Florence added, winking at Polluto. "So the night's not a total loss."

"Eee!" Petey squealed.

Elias sat at the table across from Gwen and her maps. "Gwen, I know that we've had our clashes in the past. I didn't exactly welcome you to the Jigtallica community with open arms, and I'm sorry. But—"

"Elias, all you've done tonight is create risk to serve your own ego," Gwen interrupted him. "The results were devastating, and nothing you say can mitigate that. I never want to speak to you again, statistically unlikely as that is, given that we both live in a town of less than 2000 people."

"You're right," Elias said. "I'm no better than my old man was. I put my own fiddling ahead of everyone else, and I'm sorry. I didn't listen to any of you, and I pressured you into this whole thing. But now I have my chance to make it right, and I'm taking it. I'll steal a dory and row out there alone if I have to, but I'm going to Locke-port and busting Angus Junior out of there!"

"And I'm going with ye," said Rick. "I got things brewin' back in Lockeport."

"We're in, too," Flo said.

"Never been first to leave a party before, ain't gonna start now," Win added.

"I can't let these fine ladies go to a town like Lockeport unescor-ted," said Polluto. "I be going, too!"

"Me too, boss!" said Petey. "This is just the kind of thing I've been wanting us to do together!"

Everyone cheered, except for Gwen.

"Elias, your apology is just an outlier," she said. "The overwhelm-ing trend still points to you being dangerous and manipulative. In fact, I suspect that you care more about getting your bottle back from Rita MacMurphy than you care about Angus Junior. But, con-ducting two separate rescue operations has little chance of suc-cess. So you leave me with no choice but to join you. I suppose it's possible that the irreversible brain damage you suffered from be-ing underwater for so long has made you kinder. But if it turns out you're up to something, I will throw you back in the ocean and en-sure you don't come out this time!"

"Irreversible what?" Elias asked. "You know what, never mind. I'm happy you're coming. Angus Junior seems to like you a lot, so I should make an effort to figure out why."

The first mate entered the galley, carrying a big stack of papers with him. "Hey, is there any coffee left?" he asked. "I'm gonna be up all night with this report."

"It'll have to wait," Elias told him. "We need you to take us to the captain, right away."

"Why? What is it now?"

"We need a ride to Lockeport."

The first mate stared blankly for a moment, not fully able to comprehend Elias' audacity. "You know what, why not? Knock yourselves out," he finally said. "I am so done with this stupid voyage."

Elias left the galley and sprinted down the passageway to the captain's cabin. If he could convince both Gwen and the Sea Gods to give him a chance, he was confident he could talk the *Creamer* captain into doing it, too.

23: Cream journal

The following entries from the *Theresa E Creamer* First Mate's Log from October 28th, 1922 have only recently been made public. They have been inserted here to corroborate the events of our story.

06:00 - New throater recruited.

06:06 - New throater abandons ship.

06:07 - Revenge is vowed upon new throater.

07:00 - Officers' meeting to discuss voyage objectives. Boatswain's opening remarks include a comment made in jest about leaving his new gas stove on at home. Other officers laugh, but Captain slams his fist on the table, then stands up and anxiously paces around the cabin.

07:20 - Captain begins his remarks. They are vague and incoherent, with many long pauses and references to the dangers of being forgetful, his new stove, and the unseasonable dryness of the woods surrounding his home.

07:25 - Boatswain confronts Captain about being distracted. Captain vehemently denies the charge and adjourns Officers' Meeting.

07:45 - Captain found in crow's nest, peering in the direction of Lunenburg through spyglass. When asked by Boatswain if he would like to suspend the voyage to go home and check his stove, Captain declines, claiming to be "pretty sure" it's fine.

07:48 - Boatswain reminds Captain that the further out we are, the harder it will be to turn around. Boatswain once again asks if the Captain would like to postpone the voyage. Captain once more declines, and once more begins pacing and shouting unintelligibly.

14:00 - Dories are dropped. Captain overhears Senior Throater Polluto utter the phrase "Now we're cooking with gas!" and severely reprimands him. When questioned by Boatswain, Captain enters his quarters and asks not to be disturbed.

15:00 - Captain emerges from his quarters and orders the ship turned around. When questioned by Boatswain, Captain insists the order was given because of wind conditions. Boatswain reminds Captain that it is now a ten-hour sail to our port of origin. Captain quickly resorts to name-calling and returns to his cabin. *Theresa E Creamer* turns back for Lunenburg.

15:30 - An exploratory committee is formed, consisting of Boatswain, First Mate, and Chief Engineer, to research pros and cons of a potential mutiny.

23:00 - Off the coast of Mersey Point, midway between Lunenburg and Lockeport, a dory is spotted off the starboard bow. Four survivors are brought aboard the *Theresa E Creamer*.

They are identified as Rickstopher Hirtle, Gwendolyn Risser, Florence Wentzell and Winifred Wentzell.

SPECIAL NOTE - The immediate physical attraction between Senior Throater Polluto and Florence Wentzell is so profound, it is sensed immediately by every crew member and officer. Emotional matters are not often recorded in the official logs, but the romantic chemistry between these two is so palpable that it has an intangible, yet undeniable effect on the energy onboard. While it cannot be empirically quantified, no report of this voyage could be complete without mentioning it.

23:05 - Dory survivors inform the crew that former throater Elias Oickle remains lost at sea. As stated above, revenge was vowed upon him at 06:07, causing heated debate about whether or not to conduct search and rescue. However, Haddock Randy policy definitively states that since Elias did not officially rescind his position as throater, he remains a member of the *Creamer* crew. Therefore, his rescue outweighs any vowed revenge.

Polluto assures Florence Wentzell nothing bad will happen from now on as long as he's around. He takes a dory to find Elias Oickle. Chief Steward Petey joins, citing his passion for helping.

23:15 - Throater Elias Oickle found alive. According to Chief Steward Petey's report, a heroic tracheotomy was performed by Senior Throater Polluto. No medical evidence supports this claim.

23:20 - Throater Elias Oickle knocks on Captain's door, gives a rousing speech about the meaning of friendship, and asks for passage to Lockeport. Passage granted, provided Throater Elias cuts enough fish throats to empty a dory.

23:25 - Course set for Lockeport. Senior Throater Polluto and Chief Steward Petey granted paid leave on the condition that, upon completion of *Bluenose* rescue, they return to Lunenburg, check the Captain's stove and maybe water the houseplants every few days.

23:55 - Petey, Polluto and the survivors disembark in dories a mile off the coast of Lockeport. The *Creamer* crew disavows all knowledge of this operation.

00:00 - Mutiny exploratory committee dissolved. Citing a newfound respect for the power of love and fellowship, Boatswain, First Mate and Chief Engineer unanimously vote to cut the Captain some slack for the rest of the voyage.

24: The mayor may not believe in the rule of law

The drugs still had a firm hold on Angus Junior as the *Bluenose* was tugged into Lockeport Harbour. While Elias' near-drowning had given him an hallucinatory space to work out some issues, Angus Junior had no such luck with his near-overdose. He awoke from a dreamless sleep, unaware of his surroundings, barely able to process shapes and sounds.

"Would one of you be a dear and rouse this inebriated child?" Rita MacMurphy asked Mugsy and Tony. "Or at the very least cover his face? His glassy eyes and ghastly moaning are simply too much."

"Wake up, kid. We're here," Tony said, nudging Angus Junior where he lay on the deck.

Angus Junior struggled to sit up. "Who are you?" he asked. "Uh… and who am I?"

"Well, I certainly understand not knowing who he is, but not recognizing me?" Rita said. "Something has gone badly askew in his brain if he's forgotten Rita MacMurphy."

"Lord thunderin', Mugsy. How much did you give this kid?" Tony asked.

"Just a little snootful, see?" Mugsy said. "Ain't my fault the kid can't hold his laudanum."

"Sir, I wish you'd reconsider these kinds of operations," Tony told the mayor. "Your re-election campaign is going just fine without them. You're just opening yourself up to potential blow-back."

"Says you, ya applesauce! This is the biggest score of my career, see?" Mugsy yelled back.

"Enough, the both of you!" shouted the mayor. "Mugsy, next time you drug a kid, go a little easier. Tony, quit complaining and make yourself useful. Write me a speech about how I brought the *Bluenose* back to Lockeport. Maybe say I won it in an arm-wrestling contest."

"I'm not sure people will believe—" Tony started.

"They'll believe what I tell them to believe!"

The *Bluenose* came to a stop at the Lockeport wharf, and the tugboat captain got to work securing her to the dock.

Rita surveyed the small coastal town where she was condemned to spend the night. "I can see why no one wants to come here, darlings," she said. "This town looks positively dreadful."

As the tugboat captain set up the gangplank, a flashbulb went off. Then another, and another. A gaggle of reporters had been waiting on the wharf for the mayor's arrival.

"Wow! Look boys, it's Rita MacMurphy!" a reporter yelled.

"My rate is two dollars a photo, darlings!" Rita yelled. "Ten cents extra if my feet are visible."

"Here to sing for the Mayor's birthday, Miss MacMurphy?" a reporter asked.

"I'd rather drink poison, darling. I'm simply here to repay a gambling debt."

"You forgot to cancel my birthday party?!" the mayor angrily whispered to Tony, as he smiled and waved at the reporters.

"I didn't forget," Tony answered. "Voting is less than a week away. Everyone in town just got an invitation to an open bar event with your picture on it. Do you understand what would happen to your electoral prospects if we cancelled at the last minute?"

The mayor craned his neck and looked down the street to his seaside speakeasy, East Side Mayor's. Sure enough, there was a long lineup of people in birthday hats outside.

"Gah! Elections!" he grumbled. "I'm banning them after this one!"

"What's that about elections, Mr. Mayor?" a reporter asked.

"Nothing, boys! Just happy to be back in Nova Scotia's greatest town after a little fishing trip!" the mayor yelled back.

He hopped onto the wharf, smiling for the reporters as another flurry of flashbulbs went off.

"How come you're fashionably late for your own party, Mr. Mayor?" asked a reporter. "Did you have some big deals cooking out of town?"

"Right as always, boys!" the mayor answered. "The people's work doesn't stick to a schedule, and neither do I. That's a great question."

As Mugsy and Tony helped Angus Junior down the gangplank, he stared directly into the camera flashes, drooling and twitching.

"Who's that drugged teenage boy you've got with you, Mr. Mayor?" asked another reporter.

"Just a young addict I found at sea. But rest assured, I've only brought him back here to be processed and deported from Lockeport right away. Lockeport is for Lockeporters! You can quote me on that."

"Wow, is that the *Bluenose*?" asked another.

"On the record, no comment. Off the record, yes. I won the *Bluenose* in an arm-wrestling contest," the mayor answered, winking at Tony. "I'll have details during my big speech tonight, boys! Hope to see you all there."

As Rita and the mayor walked through the crowd and approached a waiting car, one more reporter shouted, "Mr. Mayor, how do you respond to the charges that you've been embezzling municipal funds and gambling them away?"

All the reporters fell silent.

The congenial smile fell away from the mayor's face as he turned back to face the press. "Why would you ask me that on my birthday?"

"He's new, Mr. Mayor, he was just kidding around," another reporter pleaded. "No one's going to print anything like that, don't worry."

"Oh, I know you won't," said the mayor. "I just want to make sure he knows it, too. Lockeport doesn't need nosy newspapermen poking around where they don't belong."

The mayor approached the insolent reporter and put his arm around him. "Maybe you'd feel more at home reporting at the bottom of the ocean. I hear they've got a heck of a newsroom down there," he whispered. "Lots of big, tough journalists like you have left the Town Hall beat and started covering underwater stories. Mugsy here has handled all their transfers personally."

Mugsy smiled and cracked his knuckles. The reporter gulped and nodded.

"Now, with that in mind," said the mayor, "are there any more questions?"

Everyone looked away from the mayor.

"When are we?" Angus Junior asked, after a long pause.

"We're at the dawn of a new Lockeport, young man," the mayor answered. "Now, I've got a shindig to get to and a big speech to make. Come on by and have a drink, boys. You won't be disappointed!"

All the reporters smiled as the mayor got into a waiting car.

"Darlings, I'd just like to reiterate for the record that I am not here socially, nor would I ever spend time in this dump if I were not under duress," said Rita, getting in the car with the mayor. "Ta-ta!"

Mugsy and Tony helped Angus Junior into another car, and the multiple vehicles drove to a place that was less than three blocks down the road. That's just what people in small towns do.

25: Scenic Lockeport

Lunenburg's amphibious invasion of the Lockeport peninsula was launched shortly before midnight. To avoid the all-seeing eyes of local lighthouses, Gwen navigated the two dories around the far side of the unfortunately-named island of Bangay's Hole. From there, the seven commandos made their landing on Crescent Beach, a jellyfish-infested patch of gritty sand along the only road connecting Lockeport to the rest of Nova Scotia.

After everyone was on the beach, Petey and Polluto hid the dories behind a pile of debris as the Wentzells lit cigarettes and supervised.

Elias put his hand on Rick's shoulder. "What are you sayin' about how it feels to be home?"

"Ain't too bad," Rick answered.

Rick had come to get Angus Junior back for Elias and Gwen, and get the *Bluenose* back for Lunenburg. He was beginning to think about getting Lockeport back for himself.

"We got a good job of work ahead of us, we ought to start headin' er," he said.

Everyone crept along the beach to the intersection of Locke Street and Gull Rock Road, where the calamitous ERECTED FOR THE SEAMEN statue still stood. Rather than tearing the embarrassing monument down, the mayor had let it stand as a reminder of what happens to people who betray Lockeport's trust. It remains there to this day.

"Hah! Erected!" Florence yelled. "It's even funnier seeing it for real."

Everyone snickered again, but the laughter was nervous.

The only path to Angus Junior and the *Bluenose* ran through the black heart of downtown Lockeport. There are only about a dozen streets in town, but the layout is vastly more confusing than Lunenburg's near-perfect grid design. It would be up to Rick to guide the rescue party through the Byzantine labyrinth, using all the skills and knowledge of a guy who's from there.

"Listen up, me old trouts. I's only gonna say this once," Rick whispered, as they crept along Hall Street. "This flower shop here used to be the post office. Now the post office is uptown where the laundromat used to be."

"Interesting! Thanks for telling us," Elias whispered, pointing at a stationery store. "What did that used to be?"

"Used to be an all-night coffee shop called Locke Porton's," Rick answered. "Me and the b'ys used to spin yarns there til the wee hours."

No matter what the situation, it's never a bad time to talk about things that used to be other things in your hometown. Everyone always enjoys hearing that kind of valuable context.

After Rick's informative tour of downtown, the covert strike force reached a fork in the road, where Upper Water Street split off into North Water Street. Again, Lockeport is poorly laid out, especially compared to Lunenburg.

"Alright, me sons and me girl sons," Rick said, pointing to Upper Water Street. "Up there's the waterfront. They been keeping boats there for as long as I can remember."

"Gwen, lemme take a gander through your spyglass," said Elias, as he started climbing on another pile of debris. "I wanna see what the security situation's sayin'."

Gwen didn't like Elias telling her what to do, but she preferred it to climbing up the rickety stack of trash herself. "Just so you know," she said as she passed him her spyglass, "this pile of debris is very likely to collapse."

That was exactly what Elias needed to hear. This was now both a reconnaissance mission and a heat check. If he could survive this unnecessary risk, he'd know that his streak was back on, and he could once again do no wrong.

He gingerly climbed up the pile and looked out through the spyglass. The *Bluenose* was moored to a dock, but there was no sign of Angus Junior. Her deck was empty, and the only person in sight was a middle-aged tugboat captain wandering around on the wharf.

"The guard doesn't look like a problem, but I dunno if Ang-Ju is on the boat," Elias told the team.

Everyone went quiet as they heard a loud cheer in the distance.

Elias turned his gaze to North Water Street. At a speakeasy down the road, he could see the mayor and Rita MacMurphy stepping out of a car in front of a big crowd.

"Looks like Rita and the mayor are having a rager," Elias said, climbing back down. "Ang-Ju's not exactly great at parties. So we better hurry."

"How do you know where Angus Junior is?" Gwen asked. "You didn't see him. It's equally likely that—"

Elias jumped down off of the pile of debris. It did not collapse: his luck had returned. "Trust me, Gwen. Ang-Ju is there. I can feel it. I say we slip in there, sneak him out and boot 'er out of town."

"Lockeport only got one road in and out," Rick cautioned. "Soon as they see Angus Junior's missing, they'll shut 'er right down. Only other way out's by sea."

"Gwen, you take a team to the *Bluenose*, take 'er over and get 'er good to go," Elias said. "I'll take a team to the shindig and we'll meet you guys on the way out."

"Unacceptable," Gwen said. "I'm not letting you out of my sight. All your priors suggest that you'll abandon us to get your bottle back from Rita MacMurphy and ask her for music industry advice all night."

"You three go get Angus Junior, we'll take care of the *Bluenose*," offered Winifred, breaking the stalemate. "No way a Lockeport party's gonna be good. Their music is lame and the weed out here is all seeds and stems."

"I ain't never turned down a rager before, but tonight I'm more into an intimate party," said Florence, winking at Polluto.

"Aye, aye!" Polluto lustily growled. "Ye go on ahead. We'll take the *Bluenose* back from these bilge rats."

"Good thinking, boss!" said Petey. "We don't know what Angus Junior looks like, but we sure know about boats. You're smart!"

"Are you sure you can handle it?" Gwen asked. "With wind conditions as they are, you'll need to ensure—"

"Girl, we can handle it. You go French your boyfriend!" Winifred interrupted. "We snuck our way on there before, didn't we?"

"Plus, this time we have these big, strong sailors with us," Florence added, giggling.

"Did you hear that, boss? She said we're strong!" Petey said. "I told you those calisthenics were paying off. You look great!"

Gwen and Elias nodded to each other, then the whole group put their hands in a circle. "Now, let's crash this party!" Elias whispered.

And with that, everyone raised their hands and gave a quiet cheer before the group split in two. Polluto, Petey and the Wentzell sisters headed toward the *Bluenose*. Rick, Gwen and Elias started down the road to East Side Mayor's.

"Me old trouts, if this thing goes sideways, there's something I want you all to know," Rick said. "That dry goods store up the street used to be a Chinese restaurant. It was pretty good. I ain't sure why they closed it."

"Oh neat, thanks for telling us," said Elias.

In Nova Scotia, there's never a situation so urgent that a little tidbit of local trivia isn't welcome.

26: Ransom? I can hardly hear 'em

When he first got elected, the mayor had really enjoyed running his bootlegging operation out of Lockeport Town Hall. Visiting gangsters always got a kick out of it, and bullying the wimpy civil servants in the office made him feel like a big man.

But the novelty soon wore off, as keeping track of who was a contract killer and who was just a town contractor became an administrative burden.

The mayor needed a separate crime venue. So, on the final day of World War I, he invoked his emergency war powers, confiscated the Lockeport High School gymnasium, and used a team of oxen to pull it across town to the waterfront. The next day, it reopened as a gin joint named East Side Mayor's and hosted the wildest Armistice party in Shelburne County.

He kept the decor pretty much the same, but replaced the bleachers with a bar area and converted the boys' locker room into a private office. Black-soled shoes were still not allowed.

Now, at the end of his term, it was the scene of another make-or-break night for the mayor's political fortunes. With Lockeport in the midst of a tough economy and a debris-pile-related tetanus epidemic, reelection was not a guarantee. Only about 45% of the electorate could be intimidated by threats and blackmail; the swing voters who made up the 6% margin of victory would have to be won over with good old fashioned politicking.

As the mayor's chief campaign strategist, Tony had made the

birthday event crucial to his re-election strategy. Invitations had gone out, a band had been hired, and a veritable who's who of Lockeport high society had been promised face time with the mayor. But all of Tony's careful planning had gone out the window earlier that day, when Mugsy sent a telegram about a scheme to steal the *Bluenose*.

Since the day of Rick's exile, the mayor had become obsessed with the loss of the *Bluenose* contract. He had bribed all the right people, and yet he was humiliated in front of all his constituents. The job and glory all went to Lunenburg, just because it happened to be a better town.

Worst of all, it was a clear and undeniable illustration of the fact that the mayor's authority only extended as far as Lockeport's town limits. But after tonight, all that would finally change. This time, he'd let nothing get in his way.

"Sorry I'm late, everybody. One of these days I'll get a spare key to this place," the mayor said, unlocking the club's front door. "I have a big announcement to make tonight. I should wait until I've got all my Is dotted and Ts crossed, but it's going to put Lockeport back on the map, and wipe Lunenburg off of it. But first, let's get everyone nice and pliable. Who's up for a drink, on the house?"

The mayor opened the door and everybody stampeded inside too fast for him to glad-hand them.

After the crowd had filed in, Rita put on dark glasses and a head-scarf and stepped out of the car. She and the mayor discreetly walked to the stage entrance, where Mugsy and Tony were waiting with a barely-conscious Angus Junior.

"Uh...can I sit down for a second?" he asked. "Oh God, *can I?*"

"He's turning green, Mr. Mayor," Tony said. "I think the kid needs medical attention."

"Don't get hinky, Mac! He's just a bit zozzled, see?" Mugsy said. "He'll be hotsy totsy and jitterbugging again before you can say clip joint cabbage clam."

"Ever since you started reading those books about Al Capone, I can barely understand half the things you say," the mayor told him as he opened the stage door.

"What? No, you got me all wrong, see?" Mugsy said. "I've been beating my gums like this since the day I was born, see? It ain't a put on! Shmaa!"

"Absolute flops, every last one of you," Rita muttered, as they went inside.

The kidnappers and their kidnappee sidestepped the stage and made their way across the gym floor. The free drinks had started flowing and no one was going to slow the party down by turning their heads to look at a drugged-up teen.

"This constitutes a big event in Lockeport, does it, darling?" Rita asked. "And I thought Lunenburg was mundane."

"Our simple Lockeport ways may not seem like much to you, Miss MacMurphy, but step into my office," the mayor said. "Tonight, you're going to witness heritage in the making."

As the mayor opened the locker room door, a puff of steam hit him in the face. His spacious office was now completely cluttered with twenty-gallon bootleg rum stills. The bathtub-sized contraptions rattled and hissed.

"Hey nonny nonny and a hotcha cha! Get an eyeful of these twisted tubs of tiger milk!" Mugsy exclaimed.

"I'll give you the name of my decorator, darling," Rita said, lighting a cigarette at the end of a long holder. "This space is simply not functional."

"Please don't smoke around these, they're very combustible," Tony cautioned. "Sorry, Mr. Mayor. The Fire Marshal said we couldn't have these stills in the building during a gathering of fifteen or more, so I had to hide them all in here."

The mayor made a mental note to abolish the office of Fire Marshal. "Why didn't you put them in the girl's locker room?" he asked.

"We did. All the really big ones are in there. These ones are just the overflow," Tony said. "You're not mad are you, sir?"

The mayor gingerly made his way to his desk, sidestepping the whistling pipes and rattling pots and buckets. Everyone carefully crowded themselves into the room, trying to ignore the loud, volatile machines that surrounded them.

"So, we should keep things tight. Mingle for about ten minutes, then do your big speech," said Tony. "Everyone claps, I bring up the band for an hour or two of dancing, everybody goes home happy and ready to vote for four more years of fun in Lockeport. Now, Ernie 'Bingo' Hebb is gonna want some face time about driveway permits, but I told him—"

"Tony, when I'm in my crime office, I focus on crime," the mayor interrupted, sitting at his desk. "We'll deal with this governance stuff later. Now, if you'll all just give me a damn second—"

Angus Junior interrupted him by loudly vomiting into one of the stills.

"That's it! Everyone out!" the mayor yelled. "Go! All of you! Mugsy, have the kid cleaned up and back in here in five minutes."

"What should I do?" Tony shouted, over the loud distilling and vomiting.

"I said get out of here!" the mayor yelled. "God, I can barely hear myself think!"

After his associates had filed out of the crowded room, he composed himself and picked up the phone on his desk. "Operator!" he said. "Get me Captain Angus Walters."

No one knows how it worked, but back in those days if you wanted to get ahold of someone, you just picked up a telephone and said "Operator! Get me..." and then a person's name. After that, a bubble-gum-chewing lady somewhere plugged some wires into some holes and then a phone rang wherever that person was.

Fresh off Halifax Harbour's new rub and tugboat, Angus Walters Senior was getting straight up ripped at The Old Triangle pub. A telephone was brought to his table, and the receiver was placed under his ear, as he struggled to keep his head up.

"Ahoy?" he yelled. "World's fastest Captain speaking! Who's this?...Mayor of what port?...You have my what?"

"Lockeport!" the mayor yelled into the phone. "We have your son!"

"Fun? Yeah, I'm having fun!"

"What?" yelled the mayor. "No, your son! Son!"

"Bison? You got the wrong number, I'm a fish guy, not a cattle guy."

"Seattle Guy? What? I'm gonna put you on hold for a second."

"What?"

It was becoming clear to the mayor that 1920s telephones did not have sharp enough audio quality for two people in loud nightclubs to have a clear conversation. Still, he had to press on.

Mugsy brought Angus Junior back into the office, and gently helped him make his way through the vibrating stills.

"I have your son!" the mayor screamed into the phone. "Sign over the *Bluenose* tonight, or this is the last time you'll hear his voice!"

"Sorry, didn't catch that. I was ordering a drink. Who is this again?"

The mayor slid the phone to Angus Junior, who was leaning unsteadily against the desk. "Here, your pop's on the phone. Say something to him. Be loud!"

"Uh... Hello?" Angus Junior said into the phone.

"Who is this?"

"I don't know who I am anymore!"

"Hey, you sound kind of like—"

Angus Junior interrupted him by loudly vomiting again, this

time all over the mayor's desk.

"Jesus, kid! Come on!" the mayor yelled and grabbed the phone. "Sign over the *Bluenose*, or we'll kill your kid, understand?"

"Absolutely, I will!" Captain Walters said, to someone behind him asking if he'd do shots. "Okay, I'm gonna let you go. Nice talking to you!"

"Wait!" the mayor yelled. "I haven't told you where to...Ah, he hung up. We can hammer out those details later. Important thing is, I got to yes."

The mayor quickly sanitized his desk, then made another call. "Hello, operator? Get me the mayor of Gloucester, Massachusetts.... Hello, Mr. Gloucester Mayor. Tough break for your town, losing the Fisherman's Cup race, eh? That makes two in a row now, doesn't it? Well, you may be interested to know that the *Bluenose* is under new management. And maybe she might start losing a few races. What might that be worth to you?...Hmm, now that's a very interesting number. Throw in a couple shipments of guns and ammunition and you've got yourself a deal....Okay, great. Be talking to you."

He hung up the phone, took a bottle of dark rum from his desk drawer and enjoyed a celebratory swig. With something he could interpret as a verbal contract giving him ownership of the *Bluenose*, his oldest score was settled. And with a shipment of weapons on the way, his plans for the future looked brighter than ever.

He clapped his hands together, then looked out the porthole window at the crowded gym. "I guess I'd better go mingle," he decided.

"What about me, see?" Mugsy asked. "Any maroons in the crowd you want me to beat up or rub out?"

"Nah, you're good. Just watch the kid," the mayor answered, gesturing to Angus Junior where he lay on the floor. "If he stops breathing...I dunno, throw some water at him or something."

27: The Back Alley Diddlers

Because East Side Mayor's had not existed in Lockeport when he was growing up, Rick was inherently skeptical of it. Rather than approach the venue head on, Gwen and Elias hid behind a building on North Water Street, while Rick stuck his head around the corner and peered at it through Gwen's spyglass.

Fresh off his phone call, the mayor was holding court at the front door, greeting latecomers as they entered. There would be no sneaking past him.

"Really counting on that vote, Stu," he said, shaking someone's hand. "Sorry to hear that your wife died of, uh…"

"Diphtheria," Tony whispered in his ear.

"Diphtheria, right. That's a tough one. So sorry for your loss. Hey, I've got a big announcement about the *Bluenose,* though, so keep that in mind next week at the polls."

Rick watched this exchange with mixed feelings. Sure, Tony had stolen the *Bluenose* for the man who had banished him. But who among them hadn't stolen the *Bluenose* that night? Plus, he had a steady government job that he clearly excelled at. Maybe Rick should just be supportive.

"What are they sayin', Rick?" Elias whispered.

"I can't hear what they're sayin', me son."

"What are you sayin' about what you're seeing?"

"Mayor got himself planted right at the front door," Rick said, handing back the spyglass. "Ain't no way we can slink past."

"Hmm, is there a 24-hour costume store in town?" Elias asked.

"Not since the war," Rick answered.

"It's likely there's another entrance somewhere," Gwen said. "Think, Rick; what did this place used to be?"

"I don't remember there being anything on that spot…" Rick said, focusing intensely. Having been away from the peninsula for so long, his finger on Lockeport's pulse had grown weak, "But…it kinda looks like the old high school gym."

"That would explain the big hole we saw in the side of the schoolhouse," Gwen reasoned.

"The old gym had a back door onto 'er, where me and the Smoggy Boys used to smoke reefers," Rick remembered.

"What else was back there?" Gwen asked. "Were there windows? A fire escape?"

"Gwen, me girl," Rick said with a shrug, "if you remember the door behind the gym, you wasn't really there. Okay, follow me. I knows a shortcut we can creep around to 'er."

"Before we go any further, we need to address the fundamental flaw in our rescue plan," Gwen said. "It accounts for how to get in and out of Lockeport, but Angus Junior's actual extrication is completely left up to chance."

"Exactly," Elias said. "Gwen, you deal in charts, statistics, and the kind of math stuff that I don't get. I gotta give you credit, that's what we needed to get us here. But in the middle of a scheme like this, thinking about the odds won't help. We just gotta take a chance and hope an opportunity comes along."

Gwen took a deep breath. She wasn't reassured *per se*, but she did have to acknowledge that the risk involved in following Elias was equal to or greater than staying put.

It did not take long for Elias' opportunity to present itself. As they crept into the alley behind the bar, they came upon a man passed out on the pavement. He had a bottle of Mayor's Mark

Bootleg Rum in one hand and a fistful of free drink tickets in the other.

Elias knelt down to get a closer look. "Jumpin' Jesus, it's Tommy Diddler!"

"Found him, Mr. Joudrey!" shouted a Diddlin' Fiddler. "Sorry about this!"

The three-piece combo, the Diddlin' Fiddlers, approached, along with Lockeport concert promoter Ian Joudrey.

Gwen and Rick got ready to flee, but Elias smiled. "Showtime," he whispered to himself, then quickly stood up, slicked back his hair and greeted them with a big smile.

"Oh, hey, it's The Diddlin' Fiddlers! What are you boys saying?"

"Shut up, Elias!" said one of the Fiddlers. "Joudrey, we're still getting paid, right?"

"What? No! Your contract says pay to play, not pay to hang around drinking in the alley!" Joudrey snapped.

"But we came in all the way from Mahone Bay!" said another Diddlin' Fiddler. "It's not our fault the gig started late."

"It's not my fault your band leader couldn't keep it together during the delay!" Joudrey answered. "Look, I don't need excuses. That's the mayor of Lockeport in there. The man could have us all killed and disappeared under a pile of debris by morning!"

"Tommy sucked back a couple too many pops, did he?" Elias asked. "What a sin."

"Hey, I know you!" Joudrey said. "I saw your band out in Blue Rocks the other night. System of a Jig, right?"

"Jigtallica," Elias corrected. "And, yeah, we played my dad's funeral out there. Jigtallica's my new band, but I used to play with these guys. Anyways, you said if I was ever in Lockeport to give you a shout, but I can see you're busy."

He started to walk away.

"Hey, don't go anywhere!" Joudrey yelled. "I have a gig for you!"

"Oh?" Elias said, feigning surprise. "I might be open to that."

"What?" shouted a Diddlin' Fiddler. "Tommy'll flip when he wakes up."

"He'll never wake up if the mayor's birthday party doesn't have music," Joudrey said.

The Diddlin' Fiddlers looked down at Tommy, then back up at Elias. "Okay, fine. He can be our fill-in fiddler," one of them said. "But just for tonight. And we're not playing any of your trashy stuff. We're a classy band."

"It's called thrash, not trash, you wouldn't understand because you're just a jobber, not an artist," said Elias, all in one breath. "But, give me two comped tickets for my friends here, and you got a deal."

Ian shook Elias' hand.

"Just give us a second," Elias said. "I'll catch up."

"Be quick!" Ian cautioned him. "The mayor's speech starts in five minutes, and you guys are up right after."

Ian and the band carried Tommy back inside, leaving Rick, Elias and Gwen in the alley. "Here's the plan," Elias said. "I'll find a costume backstage to disguise myself and distract the crowd. With all eyes on me and everyone dancing, you two to sneak around and find Angus Junior."

"I should have predicted that your plan would involve playing fiddle on stage," Gwen said.

"I know what this looks like, Gwen. But I promise, this time I'm using my magnetic stage presence for the greater good."

A Diddlin' Fiddler popped his head out the stage door and tapped his watch impatiently. "Hurry up! We have to go over the set list!"

"Look, Gwen...You were right, back there on the dory," Elias said. "I got Ang-Ju into this, and this is the best way I can think of to get him out."

Gwen figured the chances that Elias was being sincere were about 55-45. She didn't see any clear alternative to giving him the benefit of the doubt, so she simply nodded and walked in the stage door.

Back at the front entrance, the mayor shook another hand. "Sorry about your son, Mr. Rafuse," he said. "Not easy when somebody, uh…" He nudged Tony in the ribs, looking for an answer. But Tony was distracted.

"Oh, uh, plow accident," he finally whispered.

"Not easy when someone has a plow accident, that's for sure," the mayor said, shaking his head. "Oh, speech time! It won't fully make up for the plow thing, but I do have a pretty big announcement!"

Out of the corner of his eye, Tony watched Rick and Gwen slink across the dance floor. He had taken the job with the mayor to try to get Rick's banishment reversed. Sure, that felt way off track now, but what could he do? If he left the mayor's administration, there'd be no one left to rein in his worst impulses.

All night long, Tony had been haunted by the choice between his corrupt boss and his mom's former lover. He could delay his final decision no longer.

28: Terry Tugboat's trials and tribulations

Terrence "Tugboat" Tanner warmed his hands over a flaming trash can on the Lockeport wharf. His vessel had pulled the *Bluenose* back to Lockeport and now he was in charge of guarding it. A bearded fifty-five-year-old man in a flannel jacket, Tugboat wasn't the mayor's most interesting henchman, but he had an impressive record of successful tugs.

"Hey there, sailor," Florence said, as she and Winifred approached. "Got a light?"

Tugboat barely looked up from the burning barrel as the Wentzell sisters held out their unlit cigarettes.

"I'm not a sailor, I'm a tugger," he muttered. "And I don't smoke. If you need a light, just use the can here."

Florence and Winifred leaned their faces into the flaming trash as seductively as someone can do that.

"My sister and I were just talking about 90s music," said Winifred. "She says it's overrated, but I think it's the best. What do you think?"

"No opinion. I grew up in the 80s," said Tugboat. "Gilbert and Sullivan were popular, but I found the lyrics confusing. I'm on duty here, so you two should move along."

Tugboat looked back at the fire. He either had a great poker face, or he was a total blank slate. Regardless, it was time for the Wentzells to pull out the big guns.

"Where's a good place to get a drink around here?" Florence asked.

"We're from out of town," said Winifred, batting her eyes.

In a place the size of Lockeport, no one is more attractive or captivating than a woman from out of town. She has an air of mystery, isn't likely to be related to you, and doesn't know you by your high school nickname.

"I don't drink much. There's a party down the street. Try there," said Tugboat, blankly.

"Maybe you could show us the way," said Florence. "We are from out of town after all."

"Yeah, you said," Tugboat muttered. "Wait a minute. If you're not from here, what are you doing here? This doesn't add up. I'm calling for help."

Tugboat opened his briefcase. Inside were 26 international maritime signal flags. He selected two and started waving them around, sending a code to anyone who might happen to be looking through a telescope in that direction.

"Hey, cut that out," Florence yelled. "It's weird!"

"Yeah, quit being a loser and just drink with us until you pass out!" Winifred added.

"It's not weird, it's how we tuggers communicate!" Tugboat said, waving the yellow and blue flags that represent the letter G. "I'm reporting you."

"Yo ho ho there, buddy!" yelled Polluto. "The lady said drop them flags!"

He and Petey approached from down the dock.

"Sorry, sir, these flags are official maritime communication devices. I can't stop waving them until my message has been completed," Tugboat said.

"Hey there, friend," Petey said. "I know Polluto here can be a bit gruff when he's tired, but he's a great guy and he means well.

Maybe you could put down the flags for a second and we can all discuss it as pals."

Tugboat kept waving his flags.

"Stop, I says!" Polluto shouted, and pushed Tugboat to the ground.

Tugboat stood up, dusted himself off, and then started waving the flags even faster.

"I warned ye!" Polluto said, and threw a punch at Tugboat.

"Atta boy, boss!" Petey yelled. "Right in the kisser!"

But Petey's praise was premature. Tugboat dodged the punch, swept Polluto's legs and got on top of him when the big sailor fell. In his career as a freelance Shelburne County tugboat captain, he'd pulled a number of barges out into the ocean where men fought to the death. He didn't get into any of the fights, but he had learned a thing or two just from osmosis.

Florence immediately jumped on Tugboat's back and started swearing at him. He swatted her off.

"Until the mayor signs off on the job, the *Bluenose* is technically still under my tug," he said. "I'm liable for anything that happens to it. All of you disperse, or I will be forced to continue punching."

"We ain't dispersin' nothin'!" Winifred shouted.

As Tugboat punched Polluto in the head again, Petey trembled with an intense rage that he'd never felt before. His lips quavered as he clenched his fists. "Stop...hurting...my...friend!" he shouted, then let out an ear-splitting screech.

Years of bottled-up feelings erupted as he ran up to Tugboat and punched him in the jaw so hard that the tugger flew backwards off the pier and into the ocean.

"Swim on home and don't come back, you hear?" Petey yelled. "If I see you again tonight, I'll sink your boat and drown your pets in a burlap sack! I'll do it, too! I'm straight up psycho! Go on! Get!"

Tugboat swam away, never to be heard from again in this story.

Petey collapsed on the wharf, panting.

"Y'ar, Petey," said Polluto. "I had him right where I wanted him! But still, thank ye."

The four of them made their way onto the *Bluenose* and started looking for The Wentzells' old liquor bottles.

"Wow, Petey, I didn't know you had such a hard hand," said Winifred. "Maybe while those two nurse each other's wounds, we can pop down below deck for a couple minutes."

"That's okay, ma'am, we can all nurse the boss's wounds together," Petey responded, picking up a bottle he had found. "This stuff helps when you're hurt, right?"

He showed Winifred and Florence the bottle, who eyed it with giant smiles. The label read "Laudanum".

"There's like half the friggin' bottle left!" said Winifred.

"We are gettin' lauddy tonight, boys and girls!" Florence yelled.

The Wentzell sisters had handsome sailors for company, half a bottle of laudanum and the whole boat to themselves. They'd been through a lot that night, but now they could honestly say it had all been worth it.

29: Hate oration in this dancery

"My fellow Lockeporters and Lockeporticos."

The mayor stood in the spotlight on the gymnasium stage, with a giant painting of himself as a backdrop. He tore up the boring speech that Tony had written for him, gripped the lectern, and spoke from the heart.

"We live in the greatest town on the South Shore, and yet this county is named Shelburne County and not Lockeport County. Why? Because for years, Lockeport has been stabbed in the back by every town, hamlet and municipality in Nova Scotia from Amherst to Yarmouth!"

Everyone had come to the event as apolitical winos, enjoying their free drinks and patiently waiting for the band to come on. But they were mostly non-college-educated white voters with various chips on their shoulders. The mayor was willing to bet they'd be open to hearing some populist rhetoric.

"For years, my predecessors stood by and let us get pushed around! When Peggy's Cove built a more iconic lighthouse than ours, we were told there was nothing that could be done. Brutal revenge was not planned, or even vowed!"

The crowd booed.

The tension in the room was thick as Rick and Gwen crept along the side of the dance floor. The place where Rick had once taken Tony's mom to the prom was now full of riled-up drunks, booing a lighthouse.

"It's highly probable that they're keeping Angus Junior in one of the old locker rooms," Gwen whispered to Rick. "Can you remember where they're located?"

Rick's memory of the place was hazy. He had been cut from the Lockeport High basketball team after only a few games for leaving too many cigarette butts in the key.

"Pretty sure it's this way here," he said, pointing toward the bar area.

"When I became mayor, everything changed. At long last, justice has come to Lockeport! When treacherous hooligans sabotaged our statue, the ringleader was found and banished! When Clark's Harbour opened a yarn store, clearly just to copy ours, it was burned down!"

Rita MacMurphy was unimpressed with the mayor's yarn arson. She was bored by politics, even radical ones. She sat at the bar and scanned the crowd for anyone who looked interesting enough to have a fight or one night stand with. When she saw Gwen and Rick heading her way, she got the sense that something interesting was about to happen.

"But that's only the beginning. Tonight, we begin a new chapter in Lockeport's glorious vengeance!"

"Well, hello, darlings," Rita said, sidling up to Rick and Gwen. "How wonderful to see you again!"

"Miss MacMurphy, we're not here socially. We're looking for Angus Junior," Gwen told her.

"I'm not here socially either, darling. And I'm afraid I'm going to have to turn you in, if only to entertain myself. Things have been getting frightfully dull, you see."

"Miss, please," Rick said. "I ain't a fancy man, but if you could see it in your heart to—"

"Yawn!" Rita interrupted. "Sorry, darlings, but if I have to listen to this speech for a minute longer, I'm just going to scream. I'm sure you understand."

She climbed up on a bar stool.

"I have brought the *Bluenose* back home to Lockeport, where she belongs! Now Lockeport will be the South Shore's premier tourist destination, not Lunenburg! For centuries to come, our streets will be lined with cute B&Bs and funky seasonal restaurants, not theirs!"

"Hey, everybody, I've got some Lunenburgers right here!" Rita yelled.

Usually a master at reading a crowd, Rita had misjudged how big an applause line the B&B thing would be, and the uproarious cheering drowned her out.

"And we won't stop there! As we speak, a shipment of American weapons is on its way across the border. And with them, we will expand Lockeport beyond Crescent Beach by force!"

Gwen knew that Rita would not rest until she was once again the centre of attention. She grabbed her leg. "Miss MacMurphy, before you turn us in, make sure you have all the facts," she said. "Rick, is there a hotel in Lockeport? I don't believe I saw one."

"No, there ain't," Rick answered.

"And if we were discovered, what did you say would happen to the only road out of town?" she asked.

"They'd shut 'er right down. Lord only knows for how long."

"Miss MacMurphy, if you turn us in, you're looking at an 85% chance of staying in the mayor of Lockeport's guest room for an entire weekend," Gwen said. "Or you can tell us where Angus Junior is and leave with us right now."

Rita considered this for a moment. She looked up at the wildly-gesticulating mayor, who was getting red in the face and spitting as he spoke.

"We will annex the rest of Shelburne County! Then Queens County will fall, then Lunenburg County! And one day Halifax itself!"

"I'll get my purse," Rita said, climbing down from the barstool. If there was a way to get out of spending a full weekend with these crazed bumpkins, she had to take it.

"Your little friend is in there," she said, pointing at the door behind the bar. "I'll meet you outside."

"Elect me Mayor For Life, and I pledge nothing short of total Scotia-wide domination! I see a future where there is no Nova Scotia. There is only Lockeport Scotia!"

The crowd began pumping their fists and chanting *Locke-port Sco-tia.*

Gwen looked nervously at Rick.

"Not all Lockeporters is like this," he said.

"The law of averages states that must be true," Gwen said. "Regardless, let's take advantage of this troubling distraction, grab Angus Junior and get out of here."

Everyone was so wrapped up in the chanting, no one noticed Gwen pick up a tray of drinks from the bar and carry it into the locker room.

"I'll cut taxes, too! Alright, thanks everybody. Remember this rage at the polls next week. We've got a sign-up sheet at the back for the Lockeport Militia. Anybody who wants a gun, just add your name and number to the phone tree. But for now, let's party! Ladies and gentlemen, I'm pleased to introduce Tommy Diddler and His Diddlin' Fiddlers!"

30: Playing today's light favourites

As the mayor spoke, Elias searched backstage for a disguise. Luckily for him, a fake beard and a pair of dark sunglasses had been left behind after The Lockeport Players' Tuesday Night Improv Jam earlier that week.

After being introduced as Tommy Diddler, he stepped on stage and took a quick look at the audience. They were drunk on bootleg rum and all fired up for the dance; the exact right conditions for thrash fiddle to thrive. If he really went for it, Elias knew he could get this audience going hard. That would show Rita MacMurphy a thing or two.

"What are you sayin' tonight, Lockeport?" he said. "I'm Tommy Diddler and these are my Diddlin' Fiddlers."

The crowd roared. Elias took a deep breath and started thinking like Gwen. If he tapped into the crowd's aggression and sent them into a frenzy, that would make things unpredictable. Unpredictability would make it harder for Rick and Gwen to find Angus Junior.

He was here on a mission, not to impress Rita MacMurphy. So, for the sake of his friend, Elias compromised his artistic integrity and settled into a set of predictable, mainstream ballads. Instead of using his fiddle to rile people up, he would use it to calm them down.

"We're gonna slow things down a bit, and keep them that way," he said, then started singing, "Sea angel, sea angel, say you'll be brine…"

In the cluttered office full of wheezing, clattering stills, Mugsy sat with his feet up on the mayor's desk, reading a *Dictionary of Hollywood Gangster Slang*.

The door swung open and Gwen walked in, carrying the tray of drinks high, to obscure her face. "Did someone in here order some alcohol?" she asked, cautiously making her way through the crowded room. "I'm a new waitress who started tonight. That may sound unlikely, but consider this: it's much less likely that a stranger would come in here and lie."

"Scram with the screwy speak, sister!" Mugsy said. "I didn't order no hooch!"

"As I said, I am new. So, it's unsuspicious that I'd make such a mistake," Gwen said. "In fact, we're so short-staffed, maybe that unconscious boy on the floor could barback. I'll just help him up."

Mugsy quickly underlined the word *horsefeathers* in his dictionary, then got up from the desk and pointed his gun. "Your loused-up excuse for a flim flam is full of horsefeathers, see?" he yelled, making his way through the rows of stills. "Wait a minute, you're that dorky dame from the *Bluenose*!"

"Put the gun down," she told him. "Shooting me is an illogical proposition. The muzzle flare has a near-certain chance of igniting the alcohol vapour in the air, causing an explosion that would kill us all. Additionally, it is highly improbable that you will even be conscious long enough to pull the trigger."

"What are you tooting about, Toots?" Mugsy asked, as Rick snuck up from behind and cracked him over the head with a bottle.

Mugsy dropped to the ground.

Gwen crouched in front of Angus Junior. "I don't know if you can hear me, but it's Gwendolyn Risser speaking!" she shouted as she shook him. "We're in a bit of a time crunch here, and it would really help our chances of success if you could please wake up!"

Angus Junior opened his eyes. He still wasn't sure who he was and he had no idea who was shaking him. But deep down he knew he wanted this girl to keep telling him what to do for the rest of his life.

Up on stage, Elias continued trudging through. He couldn't remember the last time he'd performed on stage without Angus Junior, and he was feeling his absence. "When you get caught between the moon and Halifax Regional Municipality," he sang, "I know it's crazy, but it's true…"

This kind of simple, mass-produced music usually appealed to audiences in places like Shelburne County. But the mayor's proto-fascist rhetoric was a tough act to follow and the crowd wasn't sure how to feel. People listlessly swayed around and danced a little, but they weren't really into it.

As the mayor moved through the crowd, he could sense their dissatisfaction. "Where'd you get this singer, Tony?" he asked. "Do we know him from somewheres? His music's pretty safe for a guy with such a wacky beard."

"Tommy Diddler came highly recommended, sir," said Tony. "He's the hottest ticket on the whole shore."

"Well, no more out-of-town bands from now on. Lockeport music only," the mayor said. "And they should be singing original songs about me. I'm working on one that goes something like, 'I'm a heartbreaker, dream maker, great Mayor, don't you mess around with me.'"

Tony stared blankly as the mayor pitched him lyrics.

Over the mayor's shoulder, he saw Rick and Gwen help Angus Junior stumble out of the locker room and slip into the crowd. "Excuse me a moment," he said and left abruptly.

"It's a work in progress!" the mayor called after him, then muttered to himself, "Whatever. Who cares if he likes it or not? What does he know?"

The mayor's trust in Tony would never recover from his

lacklustre reaction to his song idea.

As he was led across the dance floor, Angus Junior started piecing things together. "That little man means pee, right?" he said as they passed the men's room door. "I'm starting to remember... I'd like to visit the pee man."

Things were growing less predictable by the minute, and Gwen didn't need Angus Junior's bladder to be yet another variable. "Rick, you take him. I'll wait here," she said.

"Okay, but you better remember how a zipper works," Rick said, escorting Angus Junior into the bathroom. Gwen nervously waited by the door.

"Fun party, eh?" a man in the crowd asked her. "Wait a minute, do I know you?"

"Highly unlikely," she answered. "I'm from out of town."

The stranger gasped. Whispers began to ripple through the crowd at the speed of sound that an unmarried woman from out of town was in the room. Within moments, Gwen was surrounded by an impenetrable wall of local singles.

In the washroom, Rick steadied Angus Junior as he stood at a urinal.

Tony emerged from a stall and approached them. "You shouldn't have come here, Rick," he said. "It's not safe."

"Tony, me son... I don't wanna hurt ye. And I ain't got nothing more to say than that," Rick said.

"I'm sorry, Rick, but I can't let you take the *Bluenose*," Tony said. "The mayor needs it to make Lockeport a better place. It's what Mom would want."

Rick got in Tony's face. "Your mother wouldn't want nothing to do with none of this!" he yelled. "And if I'd known ye'd turn out this way, I never would've taken yer banishment for ye!"

"I've been trying to get you un-banished!" Tony yelled back. "But how can I change the mayor's mind if he doesn't trust me?"

"Tony, me son, I ain't got time to debate yer ethics. We're bootin' 'er outta Lockeport and that's all she wrote. Come on, Angus Junior."

But Angus Junior was already out the door. Forgetting to wash his hands was part of his amnesia.

"Mom still talks about you, you know," Tony said. "You can come home to her, Rick. You can be a Lockeport hero. You just have to look the other way and let me take the Lunenburg kid back to the mayor."

"Your ma deserves to live with a man who can live with himself," Rick said. "And if I done that, that wouldn't be me."

He stepped out of the bathroom and scanned the crowd for Gwen and Angus Junior, but he couldn't see them anywhere. Gwen was still completely surrounded by single men, and Angus Junior was confused and scared, stumbling around, barely able to walk. At a Lockeport dance, this actually made him blend in pretty well.

"Watch where you're going, kid!" the mayor shouted as someone stumbled into him from behind.

This was the last straw. Since his rapturous speech, things had been going downhill fast. The band was lacklustre, Tony didn't care for his song idea, his celebrity guest was nowhere to be found, and now he was getting bumped by a commoner. He decided to wait out the rest of this party in his office.

He stormed across the dance floor in a huff and went behind the bar. He opened the office door and saw Mugsy sitting on the floor, groggily picking pieces of glass out of his head.

"It was those Lunenburg palookas, see?" Mugsy said. "I'll murderize 'em!"

The mayor helped Mugsy up off the ground. Rubbing the back of his head, he looked through the porthole window in the office door and watched the band on stage. Now that he was looking for it, Tommy Diddler was obviously Elias in a fake beard.

"Mugsy, we've been infiltrated," the mayor told him. "Get our best guys, seal the exits, and round up the Lunenburg scum. Keep the Walters kid alive, but eliminate the rest. Do it quietly, though. Dead minors at my birthday party won't play well with undecided voters."

Suddenly a metal washer popped off one of the stills and hit the mayor in the crotch.

"Argh! Dammit!" he shouted.

On stage, Elias went through the motions of singing. "I'm more than a fish, I'm more than a boat, I'm more than some pretty face standing by a moat. And it's not easy being me."

He could play this sell-out music in his sleep, so he'd been using all his extra brainpower to keep tabs on his friends and enemies in the audience. What he saw was troubling.

Rick was looking around near the bathrooms, Gwen had completely disappeared, and Angus Junior was staggering around the dance floor like a pinball. Mugsy and Tony were making their way through the crowd, getting closer and closer to him.

From the back of the room, the mayor made eye contact with Elias and did a throat slitting motion.

"I can't do this anymore!" Elias shouted, and put down his fiddle. "Stop! Stop! I'm done playing this garbage."

The band stopped and the crowd went silent. If the jig was up, Elias would go out jigging his own way.

31: Nothing else mackerel

When the music suddenly stopped, Angus Junior looked up at the stage. He had no idea why, but the singer of the band was looking right at him.

"I'm not Tommy Diddler," the singer declared, removing his beard and glasses. "I'm Elias Oickle!"

He paused for gasps, but there weren't any. The Lockeport audience didn't really care if some guy they'd never heard of was actually some other guy they'd never heard of.

"Some people here tonight want to kill me," Elias continued, looking at Mugsy and Tony, who were elbowing their way toward the stage, "but I'm not going down without letting my best friend know how I feel. This might be the last song I ever play, so I'm playing it for him. Let's see if you Lockeport chumps can handle it!"

Elias turned to the band. "Okay, Diddlin' Fiddlers, this one's in E minor, 6/8 time. Watch me for the changes."

He turned back to the crowd. "Ang-Ju, this one's for you, buddy. I'm sorry I forgot the words before."

The Diddlin' Fiddlers shrugged and went along with it. They were the kind of band that didn't really care what songs they played. For the second time that night, Elias started playing *Nothing Else Mackerel*.

The crowd had sensed that all the previous ballads were passionless and they had responded politely, but not enthusiastically. But this one was different. This one had vigour. People stopped aimlessly shuffling around and started rhythmically swaying along with the music.

Cracks had been opening in Angus Junior's opiate-induced memory loss for a while now, but it totally flaked away when he heard Elias play. All at once, he recognized that this was a Jigtallica song, and that he was part of Jigtallica.

All the talent shows, battles of the bands, kitchen parties and jam sessions that he had played with Elias came rushing back. The time that they rode their bicycles six hours to Kentville to play a set at the Apple Blossom Festival. The time that they both ran away from home and spent all night jamming in a barn. The time that they played a variety show at the Lunenburg Legion Hall, but the bouncer wouldn't let Angus Junior in.

"Hey, what are you sayin'? We're Jigtallica. We're on the list."

"Elias, you can come in, but Junior here's gotta wait outside. If his dad finds out I let him in here, he'll hit the roof."

"Uh..."

"What are you even sayin' right now? Who gives a hoot? His dad's just a sea captain! Ang-Ju here is the best tin flute player this side of Port Hawkesbury, show some respect!"

"Uh... It's okay, Elias. I'll just go home. This was a bad idea anyway. Really, it's fine."

"No way! Your dad already ruined our rehearsals by kicking us out of his root cellar. We can't let him ruin our shows too! I'll tell you what, Mr. Bouncer, if you won't let us in, we'll just play our own show right here in the parking lot. And I guarantee, by the end of the night we'll have a bigger party out here than you'll have in there."

"Ugh, Okay. He can come in."

It was the first time anyone had ever suggested to Angus Junior that he could be something more than his popular father's un-wanted appendage.

Now, a feeling of pride and acceptance washed over Ang-Ju as he watched Elias up on stage in the Lockeport gym. The laudanum had worn off, he knew exactly who he was.

The instrumental intro to *Nothing Else Mackerel* was coming to a close, and Elias was starting to worry that he'd forget the lyrics again. All he could remember about the song was how he'd reacted when Angus Junior had first pitched it to him.

> "And nothing else, mackerel... Uh, and then the fiddle part would fade out. So, uh... What do you think, Elias?"
>
> "Honestly, it sounded like you were just listing stuff they sell at Fish Mart. No audience is gonna get this."
>
> "Gwen will get it! It's about how I usually order mackerel from her and nothing else."
>
> "You can't write a song that's just for your girlfriend. That's not what we're about."
>
> "She's not my girlfriend! Even still, why not? Why can't we write songs for girls we like?"
>
> "Because, Ang-Ju, as songwriters, we're canaries in the coal mine of society, okay? Our songs have gotta be about something! You know, like how politics are bad and stuff, or how Satan is cool."
>
> "Uh... I guess you're right."
>
> "I don't like you hanging out with Gwen so much. It's limiting your creativity. You've still got so much untapped spite for your dad, use that for inspiration instead. That's where the good art comes from, not from girl stuff."

Up on stage in Lockeport, Elias shut his eyes, took a deep breath, and sang from the heart. "So close, in line at Fish Mart. Couldn't need cod cheeks, tongues or hearts. I'll never order Arctic char. So, nothing else, mackerel," he sang.

He'd been wrong about this song's appeal. The Lockeport audience was absolutely eating it up. Angus Junior tried to get up to the stage, but none of the crowd members would get out of his way, as they swayed back and forth and held up lit matches.

Then he felt a hand on his shoulder.

"Ang-Ju, me son, ye can't be wanderin' off like this while you're all dinged up on L," Rick told him. "Been a good job of work findin' ye. Now, let's find Gwen and head 'er."

"Oh, hey, Rick," Angus Junior said. "Sorry, I'll try not to let it happen again. Wait, did you say Gwen's here?"

"Ah, got yer memory banks workin' again, did ye? Congrats. She's here, but I ain't seen her for a minute."

"I gotta get up there, Rick," Angus Junior said. "Gwen can't hear my song like this. The guy playing the tin flute isn't doing any of the flourishes!"

As a fan of both Jigtallica and young love, Rick couldn't let that happen. "I got ya, me son," he said, and lifted Angus Junior up on his shoulders.

Rick passed him along to the person in front of him and, caught up in the music, the crowd passed him along up toward the stage, just like the crowd at the *Bluenose* homecoming that morning. Angus Junior actually has the distinction of introducing crowd surfing to both Lunenburg and Lockeport within 24 hours.

"Trout I seek, and I find in you," Elias sang.

Mugsy and Tony could only watch as Angus Junior surfed his way to the stage. Mugsy tried shoving his way through the crowd, but it was no use.

"Hey, I'm swayin' here! I'm swayin here!" yelled one Lockeporter who Mugsy tried to elbow his way past.

"Frig off, Mugsy, I'm trying to slow dance with my gal!" yelled another.

"Never cared for perch, it's true," Elias sang. "Never cared for carp, I know!"

Right on cue, Angus Junior got on stage, snatched the tin flute from a Diddlin' Fiddler and started ripping the hardest tin flute solo anyone in Lockeport has ever heard before or since. For once, Elias was more than happy to play second fiddle.

"That's my boyfriend up there!" Gwen yelled. "He wrote this for me! It sounds like it's about fish, but it's really about us!"

Upon hearing she had a cool musician boyfriend, the crowd of single men around Gwen vanished as quickly as they'd appeared.

Rick smiled proudly as he watched Jigtallica. His evening of being a nurturing father figure had paid off, and he could see it up on the stage. Elias was going to be okay.

Even Rita MacMurphy, who was taking advantage of the distracted crowd to rifle through jackets and purses in the coat check for cash and car keys, had to admit that Jigtallica really had something.

Angus Junior and Elias didn't want the song to ever end. But it worked best as a brisk six-and-a-half-minute piece. Anything too much longer would verge on self-indulgence, and they were both professionals.

"And nothing else, mackerel!" Elias sang, one final time.

The crowd went wild as the song ended. Elias and Angus Junior took a bow, then hugged each other.

"Ang-Ju buddy, that solo was incredible," Elias gushed. "I admit I was skeptical of a Jigtallica ballad, but that was something else. It's not a normal ballad, it's like some kind of powerful ballad."

"You did the vocals perfectly," Angus Junior gushed back. "You don't think that lyric about perch was too much of a mouthful?"

"We'll do a full debrief after, but I think it's mostly there. Oh, and I'm glad you're okay!"

"Thanks for coming to get me, Elias."

"That's what co-workers in bands do," Elias told him.

The cheering crowd was still on their feet.

"Ladies and gentlemen," Angus Junior shouted at them, "my name is Angus Walters Junior, this here is Elias Oickle, and we are Jigtallica!"

32: Acting funny, but I don't know why

Below deck on the *Bluenose*, Hennigar had been bound and gagged for about five hours now. Certainly not his record, but long enough that he was starting to get pretty dehydrated.

The key to enduring forced confinement is to destroy your own humanity. To break yourself down to the point where nothing matters but retribution. Hennigar was getting into a pretty good groove with that until the Wentzells came aboard with their dates.

He could hear them above deck, singing their incessant drinking songs, talking about motion pictures and offering ignorant solutions to all the world's problems. He tried to ignore them and just focus on his quiet stewing. But their songs started getting stranger and their conversations got more and more abstract. When they started debating what would happen if the universe were a fish and its throat got cut, Hennigar started to find them really annoying.

Eventually the conversations got quieter, but the laughter got throatier. Late in the evening, Florence climbed below deck with Polluto right behind her, both giggling softly.

"Y'arr, baby girl," Polluto whispered. "You wanna get y'arred?"

"Y'arr I d'arr," she whispered back.

Giggling, she lit a candle, which illuminated Hennigar's face. He looked right through her with a thousand-yard stare. She screamed and blew the candle out before Polluto could see.

"Uh-oh, is there a spider down there?" Petey yelled down to

them. "I take care of those on our ship, too. Boss doesn't like them, but he's tough in other ways!"

"No, it's fine! Polluto, head back upstairs a sec, babe. I gotta freshen up and swab my poop deck. Lady stuff, ya know," Florence said.

"Are ye sure?" Polluto asked. "I don't mind—"

"I said go upstairs! Frig!" she shouted at him.

Polluto reluctantly climbed back up above deck.

"Win, come down here and help me out!" Florence shouted up.

"Ugh. Swab your own poop deck," Winifred muttered as she climbed below.

Florence lit the candle again. Hennigar really played up his creepy stare this time.

"Lord Moses!" Winifred yelped. "I forgot about this guy."

They got in a huddle and lit new cigarettes from each other's still-burning old ones.

"I don't want the guys to see we got our old school principal tied up. They'd probably think we're weird," said Florence. "I say we cut him loose. He ain't hurting nobody, and having him down here is gonna kill the mood some bad."

"Are you friggin' rimracked? He's gonna flip if we let him go." Winifred replied. "Probably stab our friggin' guts!"

"Yo ho ho, everything ship shape down there?" Polluto interjected from above.

"Babe, I am handing this!" Florence shouted back, then leaned back to Winifred. "Win, if you wanna keep him tied up, then you and Petey gotta stay down here with him. You know laudanum gets me all breezed up down there and I ain't wasting this buzz!"

"I'm breezing too, ya know!" Winifred pushed back. "How come I gotta be the one to get my buoy rung with a creepy teacher watching?"

They both sighed, then approached Hennigar.

"Okay, look," Winifred said. "We're gonna cut you loose. But only if you promise that you're not gonna take your friggin' gun with a knife onto it and start shooting and stabbing."

"And you gotta go take a walk for at least twenty minutes," Florence added.

Above deck, Petey and Polluto sipped from a tea set they'd found in a debris pile.

"I bet you're real good at kissing, boss," Petey said. "I think Win might want to kiss, so let me know if you've got any advice!"

Suddenly Hennigar charged up the stairs, bayonet in hand. He pointed it at Petey and Polluto. "Water!" he yelled.

"Come on! You promised!" Florence yelled up after him.

"Water!" Hennigar yelled again.

"Yo ho hold on a second, let's just calm right down," Polluto said.

Hennigar snatched Polluto's tea cup and chugged it, then grabbed Petey's and did the same.

"Our fancy party drinks!" Petey yelled.

Hennigar spotted the kettle. He grabbed it, felt that it was luke-warm and took a long drink straight from the spout.

"Lord liftin'!" yelled Polluto. "Go easy there, me old salt! Salt… Salt…Saaaalllttt…"

Hennigar began sweating as time slowed down.

When administered straight, as it was to Angus Junior, laudanum is a powerful anaesthetic. Lights out, party over. But Laudbods, or L-heads as they were known, had figured out that steaming it in a pot of tea affects the chemical compound, unlocking its potential as a party drug. As pioneers of Lunenburg's fledgling druggy scene, Winifred and Florence had put this knowledge to use.

As with any recreational drug, the trip is greatly affected by the user's state of mind going in. If you're in a fun partying mood, you could end up happy like the Wentzells. If you've just spent hours stewing in anger and are already deeply shell-shocked, you may end up with different results.

Hennigar stared at the tip of his bayonet. It began bending and twisting, moving on its own. Rainbow-coloured artillery shells exploded overhead. An army of pink elephants in spiked helmets paraded toward him through the fog.

"You must be y'arred right up," Polluto said. "Try not to freak out."

To Hennigar, Polluto and Petey's faces had been replaced by the rotting flesh of two Austro-Hungarians Hennigar had once drowned in a mud puddle. He started backing away, waving his bayonet wildly. "We're under attack!" he yelled. "They're dropping some new kind of nerve gas!"

Hennigar ripped off a piece of his shirt, urinated on it, and ran off into the night, smelling his own pee.

"Don't leave, mister!" Petey yelled after him. "You'll get hurt! You're too crazy!"

Florence and Winifred climbed back above deck.

"He'll be fine," Florence told them. "He's a teacher, he knows what he's doing."

"He didn't pooch the kettle, did he?" Winifred asked.

Florence picked it up. "Nah, we still got about half a pot. So, what are you guys saying? How about one more round and then we pair off and French?"

33: Fiddle 'em all

From the stage, Elias sized up the mayor's security detail. Two municipal workers in Town of Lockeport construction vests stood guard at the exit nearest the stage. Mugsy and Tony were pushing their way through the audience toward Jigtallica. The mayor stood at the main exit, brandishing a length of pipe, which was actually his trademark during voter meet and greets.

"Alright, Lockeport, we got one more song," Elias yelled as he drop-tuned his fiddle. "This one's called *Gwen and Rick Get Up Here, We're Leaving*."

"Uh, I'm not sure I know that one," Angus Junior whispered.

"Don't worry, we're just gonna jam as hard as we can. We'll start with that riff we were working on out in the shed last week," Elias told him, then yelled to the crowd, "Show me what you've got, Lockeport! I wanna see you tear it up in the pit!"

With that, Jigtallica launched into the heaviest, most anti-establishment song anyone in Lockeport had ever heard. Music this aggressive would not be played again anywhere on earth until the invention of the double kick pedal.

The crowd was already amped up from the mayor's promise of Scotia-wide dominance, they had been drinking bootleg rum all night, and now they were sonically bombarded by a reunited Jigtallica. All this energy had to go somewhere. A mosh pit was the only logical conclusion.

It started as just a handful of leaping young men, so overcome with emotion that they had no choice but to thrash around wildly. But as the feeling spread and the music got harder, drunk people all over the gym began to throw themselves at one another with reckless abandon. All the crowd members Mugsy had been trying to push out of his way began to push back.

Soon, even the cool thirty- and forty-somethings who had been just standing at the back of he room with their arms folded, nodding along with the music, were pulled into the action.

The mayor had wanted to handle things quietly, but he couldn't allow this vulgar display of fiddle to continue. He sought to harness and control the pent-up rage of his constituents, but Jigtallica's pulse-pounding arpeggios embodied a freedom so pure, they rendered all who heard them uncontrollable. Their sound was so intense, so new, that it threatened all authority.

The mayor went behind the bar and got his long, tin cone megaphone. "People, remain calm!" he shouted. "These out of town fiddle faddlers are trying to tear us apart! Stop this! Stop this, I say!"

"You can't tell us what to do! We live in a different town!" Elias yelled back.

Gwen elbowed her way through the mosh pit and climbed up on stage. "These riffs are well outside the acceptable threshold of heaviness!" she told Elias. "You're creating chaos!"

"Exactly," Elias told her.

Each time a drunk got shoved, a new array of possible outcomes opened up. The risk was growing too exponentially for Gwen to process. But in the chaos, Elias saw opportunity.

Mugsy was caught in a circle pit, leaving the mayor's security force without a leader. The Town of Lockeport guards at the stage exit fidgeted uncomfortably as the shoving spread closer and closer. This left Tony as the mayor's last best option to shut Jigtallica down.

But as he neared the stage, Rick stepped in front of him. "Tony, me son," he said, "let's both just walk away right now. We'll tell your ma the truth and we can all go back to being a family."

"It's not that simple, Rick," Tony said. "The mayor's watching. I have to get up there."

"Then ye have to go through me," Rick said.

Tony tried to throw a punch, but Rick grabbed his fist.

"Jeez, Rick! Ow!" Tony yelled. "Let go!"

Rick let go and Tony stumbled backward into a big guy in a Hawaiian shirt, causing him to spill his drink all over a nearby couple.

Elias watched from the stage. In a town like Lockeport, everyone harbours a lifetime of petty grievances against everyone else. Chances were high that there was an existing tension between at least two of these people, and they would only need the gentlest of subconscious nudges to push them into violence.

"Alright, Ang-Ju, double time!" Elias shouted, speeding up his fiddling.

Angus Junior's fingers trembled. He was already tooting the heaviest music he had ever played, to speed it up for a crowd this amped was outright dangerous.

"Elias, what is the goal here?" Gwen asked.

"If they're fighting each other, they can't fight us."

The aggressive music crept into the bloodstream of the guy in the Hawaiian shirt. It had been a room full of shoves, but he threw a punch. The Rubicon had been crossed. The mosh pit was tilting toward a brawl, just as Elias had planned.

"Stop this! Mugsy! Shut this down!" the mayor shouted from the back of the room.

Mugsy reached for his gun, but was shoved by a childhood acquaintance with a longstanding resentment.

"Mugsy, you've been making fun of my pants since 1917. Well, it stops tonight!" the man yelled.

"Your pants are way too big, see? I can't just ignore that, see?" Mugsy responded, shoving the man back. "You're yesterday's news, pal!"

With Mugsy and Tony now caught up in their own personal fights, the mayor started getting desperate. "Attention!" he yelled into the cone. "Whoever gets them off the stage will be granted lifelong immunity from all municipal bylaws, no questions asked!"

This only further incentivized everyone in the crowd to fight each other to be the first one to the stage.

Elias watched the melee as he played faster and heavier. He took special notice of the two Town of Lockeport guards at the stage exit, who dodged an errant chair flying against the wall.

"Should we be trying to break this up?" one asked, nervously watching the mayhem.

"No. We were told to stay here and watch the door, and that's what we're gonna do," said the other. "No one can get mad at us for doing what we're told."

This is why you don't hire government workers to do a criminal's job.

"They'll clear the exit soon. We just gotta hold everyone off a little longer," Elias told Gwen. Then he yelled to the crowd, "You call this a mosh pit, Lockeport? You guys can't thrash worth trash!"

A straggler climbed on stage and wobbled up to Angus Junior. Before the drunk could throw a punch, Gwen body checked him off the stage. Another straggler approached, and Gwen handled him just as easily.

Growing up with eight older brothers had given Gwen a lifetime full of data on how drunk young men fight. She used her uncanny forecasting ability to predict and counter everyone's moves as they happened. Probability of a haymaker: 85%. Probability of a two-handed shove: 80%.

"Uh, thanks Gwen!" Angus Junior said.

"Thank me later. Put that tin flute back in your mouth and blow!"

More and more crazed drunks began rushing the stage.

"There's too many, Elias!" Gwen yelled. "My chances of holding them off any longer are only one in six!"

Just then, Elias caught the lucky break he'd been waiting for. One of the Town of Lockeport security guards saw an injured man lying on the floor, and suddenly remembered how that guy had stolen his girlfriend back in high school.

"Sorry, but I have to do this," he said, leaving his post to kick the guy while he was down.

"Hey, two to an exit, that's the rule!" said the other guard, following him. "I'm not working the door by myself. That's not the protocol."

Back on stage, Elias abruptly lowered his fiddle. "Okay, we've been Jigtallica!" he shouted to the crowd. "Joudrey, we'll be in touch about future bookings!"

He started toward the exit, but Mugsy got in his way.

"Show's over, see?" he said. "I'm gonna beat you up worse than I just beat up that guy with the dumb pants!"

"Fiddle me this!" Elias shouted, and smashed his fiddle across his chin. Mugsy fell off the stage into the brawling crowd, where the big pants guy's brother was waiting for him.

"Rick, I guess we're leaving now!" Angus Junior yelled, as he, Gwen and Elias ran toward the unguarded exit. "Goodnight, Lockeport!"

34: Rick's Picks (like *Sophie's Choice*)

For most of Jigtallica's set, Rick had been patiently locked in battle with Tony. Tony would throw a punch, or give a shove, and each time Rick would softly block or dodge. His paternal bond for this man two years his junior was too strong to let him fight back.

But when Jigtallica left the stage, his patience ran out. "Tony, me son, this is your last chance," he said. "Just come to Lunenburg with me, we'll sort it out!"

"And leave Ma? If I did that, she'd have nobody!" he yelled back.

"Yeah? Whose fault is that? You wrote them damn boner words on the statue! You started all this!"

In the heat of the moment, Rick shoved Tony with all of his might. He famously had the softest hands in Lunenburg County, but now they'd been used to inflict wrath.

As he ran toward the exit, Rick felt a deeper shame than he ever had before. Which is saying a lot for a man who routinely recruited clients at their husbands' funerals.

Outside, Elias, Angus Junior and Gwen were waiting in the alley.

"Hey Rick, what are you sayin'?" Elias asked, as Rick finally made it out the stage door.

"Are all of your Jigtallica shows this exciting?" Gwen asked.

"They're usually better on a technical level, but this one had an especially memorable energy, I would say," Elias said.

"Hey, uh, Gwen, I was thinking," Angus Junior said. "In case we don't make it out of Lockeport, what would you think about maybe putting on our gravestones that we were boyfriend and girlfriend?"

"That's a sweet sentiment, Angus," Gwen replied, "but we have a very high probability of escaping Lockeport. The *Bluenose* is close by. Just through the alley, across the parking lot and then down the street, right, Rick?"

Rick paused for a second and took a deep breath. "I ain't coming with ye," he told everyone. "This here was always a one-way voyage for me, me old trouts."

"Rick, what are you saying?" Elias asked. "I admit the scheme for you to marry Rita didn't work out, but that's no reason to stay in Lockeport!"

"Back on the dory, I never should have let ye go, me son," Rick said, "but I never should've let Lockeport go, neither. Me home is here."

"But what about Jigtallica?" Elias asked. "We need you as a manager. *I* need you!"

"I seen you up there on the stage. You guys got 'er all figured out. You don't need a manager, and you don't need a fake dad. I taught you everything you gotta know."

Rick looked back inside the gym, where all the people he grew up with were beating the absolute crap out of each other. Tony was still lying on the floor, with no one there to help him up. Rick knew in his heart that Tony was going to get himself killed if he stayed in the employ of the mayor.

"I need you as a friend, Rick," Elias said. "So what if I don't need you as a dad?"

"Somebody in there do need a dad," Rick said. "And his ma needs me, too. Big time."

A horn honked from the parking lot.

"Beep beep, darlings!" Rita yelled. "I've stolen a motorcar! Let's abscond, shall we?"

"Go on now," Rick said. "You guys give 'er the gears and boot 'er on outta here with the *Bluenose*."

Gwen hugged Rick. "I'll never forget you. Your kindness makes the average Lockeporter a little bit better on aggregate."

"I ain't know what that means," Rick said, "but thank ye kindly."

"I still might get my first kiss tonight, Rick," Angus Junior told him. "If I do, I'll use all the techniques I practised on that fish head. Just like you told me."

"You really done that, eh?" Rick said. "I was just yankin' yer chain when I said to practice on one of them, but...I'm glad it helped."

Elias knew that even if he somehow convinced Rick to come with them, he'd never be happy. The fact that he was even considering Rick's feelings, and recognized that they were valid even though they were different from his own, was proof that Rick had done his job as a fake dad.

"I owe you one of these," he said, handing Rick a cigarette. "Found them in Diddler's suit jacket."

No one had ever offered Rick a cigarette before; he had always been the one to give them out.

"Goodbye, Rick," Elias continued. "Without you, I wouldn't be the man I am today. I'd still be the boy I was last week."

Rick gave Elias a hearty handshake, the equivalent of a hug in that time and place. "You've got a bright future ahead, me son," he said. "I'll write to ye as soon as I get settled. Until then, listen by your ma's bedroom door. If ye hear squeaky bed spring sounds, you'll know I'm there in spirit."

"I won't do that, but I'll look forward to your letters," Elias told him.

Angus Junior, Gwen and Elias ran down the alley, waving goodbye to Rick. He stepped back through the stage entrance. He had no scheme to save Tony's soul, but he just wouldn't be Rick if he didn't try something.

He crept along the side of the room. Without the thrash fiddle music, most of the fighting had slowed down, leaving only those with the bitterest grudges still duking it out.

"People, please," the mayor yelled through his cone, "save your hatred for the outsiders!"

Rick thought he could lay low and try to intercept Tony again in the bathroom. He'd probably been drinking enough that he'd surely have to go again. God only knew what he'd had to eat that day.

As he fretted about his surrogate son's diet and scanned the room for hiding places, Mugsy came up behind him and put his gun to his back.

"Look what the cat dragged in!" he said. "I invented that phrase, see? Now, march! Big man's gonna wanna have a little squawk with you."

Mugsy walked Rick across the floor and back to the bar.

The mayor put his cone down when he saw Rick. "Look what the cat dragged in!" he said, not attributing the phrase to Mugsy. "If I'd had the political capital two years ago, I would've killed you myself."

"How many holes do you want me to plug into him?" Mugsy asked. "What's our bullet budget on this one?"

"Let's be reasonable," Tony said. "If we leave him alive, we—"

"Cram it!" The mayor yelled. He had offered Tony his job as political advisor the day after Rick's exile. His willingness to shut his mouth and let Rick take his punishment showed exactly the kind of spinelessness the mayor was looking for.

But Tony had been on the mayor's bad side all day. He'd been a total wet blanket about the *Bluenose*-stealing operation. He'd written a boring speech about property tax cuts instead of one about taking over Nova Scotia. Most hurtfully, he was uninterested in the mayor's song lyrics.

"Mugsy, go find the others. They can't have gotten far," the mayor said. "Tony and I will take care of Rick. Won't we, Tony?"

The time had come for Tony to prove his loyalty.

35: When logic and proportion have fallen slowly dead

Since its inception, the automobile parking lot has been a place where weirdos love to skulk around on drugs. And so, like a moth to the flame, Hennigar had been drawn to the alley behind East Side Mayor's. With ample bush coverage around the perimeter and five spaces to peep at, it was the best game in town.

For a while he'd been content to wave his rifle around at the cars and yell incoherently at the street lights. The mayor's political events often attracted this type of guy, so no one paid him much mind.

Then the teens came out of the alley and piled into a car with a woman he had seen on a box of menstrual powder at the drugstore.

Hennigar had seen so many undead Austro-Hungarians recently that he'd gotten pretty good at telling what was a hallucination and what was a real enemy. These were the teens alright, in the flesh. He couldn't remember why, but he knew they had to be stopped.

He jumped out from the bushes and waved his gun around, screaming incoherently until Rita slammed on the brakes.

"Oh, hey, Hennigar, what are you sayin'?" Elias yelled. "We were just on our way to untie you."

"I've got you now!" Hennigar shouted. "Out of this driving machine, all of you!"

"Hennigar, we don't have time for this," Elias told him. "We were wrong to kidnap you, I'll admit that. But if you weren't following us around with a gun, it wouldn't have happened. Just put it down and let's talk this through."

The drugs were starting to open Hennigar's mind to the idea that violence wasn't necessarily the answer. He hated that. "You teens aren't talking your way out of this one!" he yelled. "You're destroying this country, just like the Austro-Hungarians!"

"Get it together, Hennigar! You keep ragging on us teens, but you're the one picking fights in a parking lot!" Elias yelled back. "Before you go blaming me for everything, maybe go take a look in the mirror. If you even can, your pupils are huge right now. Are you on drugs?"

"I think so! But because of you teens!"

"Blaming others yet again," Elias said. "Ugh, and you absolutely reek like pee. Miss MacMurphy, just drive around him. Let's leave him here. As a crazy guy who just wants to shoot people, he'll be right at home here in Lockeport."

Hennigar was so drugged up that he had actually listened to a student's back-talk. Was it really possible that the concerns of people over twelve and under twenty should be taken seriously? Was his all-consuming rage at their very existence somehow misplaced?

In his altered state, his neural pathways were firing too fast for him to shut that kind of thinking down like he usually did.

"Hop out of the jalopy, see? All of you'se!" Mugsy yelled.

"Aw, great," Elias muttered. "Thanks a lot, Hennigar! Now we have a real threat to deal with."

Mugsy came around the corner of the alley with his Tommy gun. "You're all washed up, see?" he yelled at them. "Shmaa!"

Maybe the drugs made Hennigar mishear the old time gangster exclamation 'Shmaa' as the Austro-Hungarian greeting 'Szia'. Maybe his army training took over and he prioritized an armed man over a vendetta against a disruptive student. Or maybe Elias' tough love had convinced him to use his rage for good instead of evil. Some combination of these factors caused Hennigar to stop pointing his gun at Elias and point it at Mugsy instead.

"Evacuate, troops!" he shouted. "I'll hold the enemy off!"

"Okay, thanks, ciao, darling!" Rita shouted, slamming on the gas pedal.

The Model T sped away as Hennigar fired wildly in Mugsy's direction.

Mugsy dove behind a wall. He'd never actually been shot at before. Like many young men of the era, he was just going through a gangland Chicago phase. He took a deep breath, then popped out from behind the wall and sprayed bullets all over the place, just like he'd practised at home.

A bullet hit Hennigar's shoulder and he fell to the ground. Since this was before the advent of penicillin, Mugsy could reasonably assume the wound would get infected and kill him. So rather than finish him off, he hopped into the mayor's second car and took off after Rita.

Hennigar lay flat on the ground with metal in his arm and the fog of war in the air, just like in the trenches. For the first time since the war ended, things made sense to him again.

He aimed his rifle and shot at Mugsy's car, hitting a tire.

As he watched Mugsy careen into a pile of debris, Hennigar was at peace with his own soul. His entire career as an educator, he had hated all teens and sought to thwart them at every turn. Now, to help a few teens, he had taken a bullet and caused a car accident. This felt karmically balanced to him.

Laudanum is a hell of a drug.

Mugsy checked himself for broken bones as he crawled out of the car. The waterfront was about a ten-minute walk away, which to someone in a small town is an unthinkable marathon. But, what choice did he have? He couldn't go back to the mayor empty handed, and by now Hennigar had disappeared into the night.

36: Blatant municipal government overreach

So far, the evening had been a net negative for the mayor's reelection campaign. While it was reassuring that Lockeport voters enjoyed extreme rhetoric and physical violence, his reputation as a man of law and order took a hit when his event devolved into complete anarchy. If he didn't stage a dramatic comeback, Lockeport Scotia might be smothered in the cradle.

The mayhem in the gym had now fully run its course. Everyone was now mending fences, logging new grievances for next time, and trying to figure out who was still going home with whom. Above all, they were heading to the exit.

Suddenly all the lights turned off, except for a spotlight on the mayor. "Ladies and gentlemen, thank you all for coming," he said. "I have one more surprise this evening, if you'll allow me. It is my birthday, after all."

"Come on, Mayor, it's 3 AM and I've got a chipped front tooth," a man in the crowd shouted back. "I just want to go home."

"We all want to go home, son," the mayor said. "I just want to make sure that we all have a home to go back to. But, unfortunately, there are dark forces out there who want to take that away from us."

The crowd began murmuring. The mayor walked through the crowd toward the stage, with the spotlight following him. Everyone was exhausted, but if the mayor could make a convincing case as to why this giant brawl had been someone's fault other than their own, they were willing to hear him out.

"Did you think it was a coincidence that those out-of-town agitators came in here to tear us apart on the very night of our ultimate triumph?" he asked. "I wish it were that simple, but the horrible truth is that Lunenburgers and Lunenburg sympathizers are carrying out a vast conspiracy against Lockeport! They are being rounded up as we speak, but we have already caught their leader!"

The spotlight swung up to the front of the room and illuminated Rick, who was tied up against the apron of the stage.

The crowd gasped. The mayor had been ranting about a conspiracy against Lockeport at every public appearance from cutting the ribbon at the new daycare to lighting the town Christmas tree. But this was the first time he had something that resembled proof.

"That's right! The statue traitor is back to finish the job!" the mayor continued. "He hates our freedom so much that he's come back to steal the *Bluenose* from us a second time."

"That ain't what's happening here!" Rick yelled.

"Oh no?" the mayor said. "Did you or did you not brainwash an innocent youth into writing lewd *double-entendres* on our town statue?"

Rick looked at Tony, who avoided eye contact. "I did," he answered.

"And were you not banished for that crime?" the mayor continued, "told never to return under penalty of death?"

"I were," he said.

"And yet you came back to incite a riot with your Lunenburg confederates!" the mayor continued.

"I didn't incite nothing!" Rick insisted.

"Then what were you trying to do?" the mayor harangued.

Rick looked back at Tony. "I come here to set things right."

"I think we can safely construe that as stealing the *Bluenose*!"

the mayor told the crowd. "The whole conspiracy traces back to him. Rick is the reason our town doesn't have anything good! Rick is the reason the only jobs available are in the bootlegging industry! Rick is the reason you all punched each other just now!"

The crowd angrily booed and hissed at Rick.

"Rickstopher Hirtle, you have confessed to crimes against Lockeport. As Mayor, I sentence you to death!" the mayor said.

Everyone gasped. Even for Lockeport, this seemed to be well beyond the jurisdiction of municipal bylaw enforcement.

"We all knew public executions were going to be part of my administration at some point, so let's not be babies about this," he said. "It's time to decide for real. Are we just little Lockeport in Shelburne County, or are we Lockeport Scotia?"

The crowd again started chanting 'Lockeport Scotia' and menacingly moving up toward the stage.

The mayor handed Tony a pistol. "Tony, you said on your resume that you work well under pressure. It's time for you to prove it."

The chants of 'Lockeport Scotia' grew louder and louder as Tony stared at the pistol in his hands.

"If you don't shoot him, you'll be up against that wall yourself!" the mayor told him. "I don't really need a political consultant anymore."

"I'm sorry," he said, and handed the pistol back to the mayor. "I can't do it."

"Why would you give it back to him!?" Rick yelled. "Thanks for not shooting me, but come on, me son!"

"I had this extra one in case you didn't do it," said the mayor, pointing two pistols at Tony. "But yeah, not sure what you were thinking there. Up against the wall. This guy's part of the conspiracy too, everyone! Don't worry about how, we'll figure it out!"

As Tony walked toward Rick with his hands on his head, the chants of 'Lockeport Scotia' grew louder.

37: Wind-related performance issues

The mayor's Model T whipped down the street with Rita behind the wheel, Elias in shotgun and Angus Junior and Gwen in the backseat. Rita took one last gulp out of a rum bottle and tossed it out the window. None of which was illegal, or even socially taboo, at that time.

"I'd usually not be caught dead in something as drab as a Model T, darlings," Rita said. "With all that bootlegging money, you'd think the mayor would drive something sporty and fun. Some people simply don't have style, I suppose."

She patted herself down for another bottle and found one on a string around her neck. She opened it and held it to her lips. "Oh, toots! I forgot this one has your dreadful fiddle arrangements in it," she said, handing it over to Elias. "They're probably more tedious than funny, so I suppose you may have this back, darling."

Elias greedily snatched his bottle. But the contents felt incomplete. "Hey, Ang-Ju," he said, turning around to face the back seat, "do you have a copy of *Nothing Else Mackerel* handy?"

"Oh, uh, yeah, I think so."

"Put it in here when you get a chance," Elias said, handing him the bottle. "It's a Jigtallica song; it belongs with the rest of them."

Angus Junior took the bottle and added some more tattered papers from his pockets to the wad inside.

The car screeched to a halt before he could pass the bottle back to Elias. The whole drive had taken less than three minutes. They absolutely could have walked.

"We're here, old sports!" Rita announced. "Now let's escape this dump, shall we?"

They stepped out of the Model T and gazed up at the *Bluenose*.

The Jigtallica boys had always just seen her as Angus Junior's dad's boat. But here in the moonlight, they saw her for the first time for the powerful icon she was. After what they'd seen and been through, they now felt the importance of getting her back to Lunenburg. Not for their own sakes, but for the sake of all Nova Scotians, they had to keep such a powerful symbol out of the hands of the mayor of Lockeport.

"Angus Junior, I estimate that Mugsy should arrive on foot in eight minutes," Gwen said as they hurried across the wharf. "That doesn't leave us much time to prep the *Bluenose* for sail."

"Oh, hey, what are you guys sayin'?" said Florence, climbing up from below deck and fixing her matted hair. "Where's Rick?"

"He decided to stay and make Lockeport a better place," Angus Junior answered.

"Good luck with that," she said.

"Dang, I wanted to brag to him about how I got laid," Winifred said, getting up off the deck.

"You can brag to us," Elias said.

"Ain't the same. You guys wouldn't understand any of the details."

Gwen took her position at the ship's wheel. "You can explain the mechanics of coitus to us later, ladies," she said. "Right now, everyone needs to get to their stations!"

"Oof, gimme a second to have a smoke first," Florence said. "I am lauded to the gills right now."

"Okay, but we really need to—" Gwen continued, as Petey and Polluto approached, tucking in their shirts.

"Hey, boss, there's Rita MacMurphy, just like I seen in town last night!" Petey yelled. "Now you seen her, too! No one has to feel left out!"

Polluto bowed to Rita MacMurphy and extended his hand as she boarded the *Bluenose*. "Yar, Miss MacMurphy! I've been a fan of yer work since *Girl Enters And Exits Building*. Ye should've been cast as the sexy robot in *Metropolis*!"

"Thank you darling. Fritz Lang and I had too many disagreements over the script," she said. "His loss, I suppose!"

"Whoa, what's Miss Priss Radio Host doing here?" Florence asked. "First she stole our booze, now she's stealing our boyfriends?"

"Don't be crass, darlings. I don't steal boyfriends," Rita answered. "Though I have been known to borrow a husband or two."

"Borrow this!" Winifred yelled, and charged at Rita.

Gwen calculated an 80% chance of hair pulling and a 90% chance they wouldn't get out of the harbour before Mugsy arrived.

Petey and Polluto held the Wentzell sisters back as Elias stood between them and Rita.

"If you could all just focus for a moment," Gwen pleaded.

"Sit your tramp rear ends down before I knock you down!" Rita chirped.

"You don't know me!" Florence shouted. "You don't know me!"

Angus Junior blew a loud shrill note on his tin flute until everyone quieted down.

"Listen up! Uh, please," he shouted, gaining confidence as he spoke. "Last I checked, this ship is the *Bluenose* and my name is Angus Walters, so that makes me the captain. So if you don't follow my orders, you can swim home! My first order is that everyone shuts up and listens to Gwen. Not just cause she's my girlfr—uh, a girl who I hopefully might date some day, but because she knows her sailing stuff! Gwen, the floor is yours."

"Thank you Angus Junior," she said. "Everyone, time is of the essence—"

Angus Junior dreamily listened to Gwen bark orders. Just as she had predicted, with a little cooperation, the *Bluenose* was unmoored and ready to go in short order. Angus Junior even untied a knot this time. He just needed the confidence.

"What are your orders, Captain?" Gwen asked.

He briefly considered ordering her to go on a date with him, but that wasn't really the note he wanted their relationship to start on. "Uh, you know, make the boat go, or however you say it. Let's go home!"

Everyone cheered as the sails unfurled.

But nothing happened. The boat didn't move an inch. The cheering gradually died down as everyone realized they were in trouble.

"Uh…" Angus Junior said, "did we do it wrong?"

"No, I just failed to account for a sudden drop in air pressure," Gwen said.

Angus Junior stared blankly.

"The wind stopped blowing," she elaborated, "so we're stuck."

"How do we fix that?"

Gwen gave a forlorn shrug. It was unfixable. Sometimes it just isn't windy enough for sails to work and there's nothing you can do. This was a big reason people started putting motors on boats.

"Uh, should we try rowing maybe?" Angus guessed.

"Y'arr, I been sailing eight years! I should be in charge instead of these high school sweethearts!" Polluto yelled.

"You do a great job being in charge of me, so it makes sense you'd do a great job being in charge of everybody!" Petey added.

"How exactly would you have made it windy, old sport?" Rita asked.

"Don't sass my man like that!" Florence yelled. "Maybe you should get out and push!"

"Maybe you should get out and push—a comb across your hair!"

Rita said. "You look offensive, darling."

Everyone started yelling at each other again. Angus Junior tried to reassert his command, but this time to no avail. He'd shot his leadership wad.

Everyone was so consumed with fighting each other, no one noticed Mugsy approaching the wharf. "Alright ya wet socks!" he shouted. "Ya can't cheese if there's no breeze, see?"

Everyone stopped arguing and looked at him.

"I been sore since settin' sail on this silly sloop, see?" he continued. "I've been bayoneted, bottled, bruised and battered, and, to top it off, I just had to take a brisk 15-minute walk! Soon as I catch my breath, I'm sinking 'er, see?"

He pointed his gun yet again, this time not a person, but at the hull of the *Bluenose* herself.

38: And our Locke become a funeral pyre

After the battle of Vimy Ridge, some teenaged soldiers in Hennigar's platoon had made a pact to lose their virginities before the war ended. When they refused to let Hennigar join, his jealousy led him to make hating teenagers a core part of his identity.

After making his narcoticized peace with teens in the parking lot, he felt more aimless than ever. As far as he was concerned, there was nothing left to do but find a place to nurse his wounds, grab something to eat, then wander into the woods and live out the rest of his days there. Who among us has not come to this conclusion while on drugs?

Hennigar staggered into East Side Mayor's in search of wilderness survival supplies or some leftover hors d'oeuvres. He found neither. All eyes were on the mayor and the unfolding drama of Rick's upcoming execution, so no one noticed Hennigar.

He made his way to the bar and treated his shoulder wound with a wad of cocktail napkins and some overproof rum.

Something about this crowd just wasn't sitting right with Hennigar. On any other night, he would have been a big supporter of executing a young man for writing a crude joke on a statue. Maybe it was the laudanum talking, but seeing a charismatic leader whip a crowd into a frenzy with chants and calls for blood was giving him Austro-Hungarian vibes. German vibes, even.

If teens weren't the real problem, maybe this kind of thing was.

Hennigar did the only logical thing he could have done as a mentally-unstable man on a powerful hallucinogenic. He took off his shirt and poured rum all over it. Then he wrapped it around his bayonet and lit it on fire, while singing an old army marching song to himself.

"You know that it would be untrue, you know that I would be a liar," he sang.

His historically accurate singing was drowned out by the chants of 'Lockeport Scotia!'

He danced around the bar, waving his makeshift torch and letting the flames drip where they may. A thousand shoves had caused a thousand spilled bootleg drinks and gave the blaze a thousand little places to spread.

By the time anyone noticed that he had set the building on fire, Hennigar was gone.

No one knows for sure what happened to him after that. Some say he died of exposure later that night. Some say he found a cave in the woods and made a nice life for himself as a hermit. Still others say he showed up for work the next day at the Shelburne County school board and they just put him in charge of a different classroom somewhere.

Regardless, his spirit lives on in the fierce passions, short tempers and bizarre personal lives of Lunenburg County educators to this day.

With their backs up against the stage, Rick and Tony were the first to see that a raging fire was engulfing the back of the gym. The bar area and the main entrance were already totally enveloped in flames.

"Any last words, Tony?" the mayor asked, pointing his handguns at them.

"Yes," Tony said. "Everyone form an orderly line at the stage door and begin evacuating! The building is on fire!"

When the mayor turned around and saw the flames, two things immediately came to mind. First, the rum stills in his office were not explosion-proof in any way. Second, he shouldn't have dissolved the Lockeport Fire Department for refusing to swear a loyalty oath to him.

"Mayors and children first!" he yelled. "After that, it's every man for himself!"

The mayor ran toward the stage exit, pushing people out of his way. Rick stuck out his foot and tripped him.

Fire spread through the gym and the horde of Lockeporters pushed and trampled one another on their way to the door. No one stopped to help the mayor.

"Stop trampling me, you fools!" he yelled from the ground, but it was no use. They trampled him good.

Maybe if the mayor would've had a bit more indoctrination time, he could have conditioned the townspeople to prioritize his safety over their own. But he'd only been in office four years and you can't rush these things.

After Tony untied his hands, Rick picked up the mayor's megaphone cone from the floor.

"Listen, me b'ys! I speaks from experience!" he yelled. "If we put our own needs first, and just grope our way through, we're all sunk. But if we just take 'er easy and all get on the same page, we'll be sliding right through that door, real easy."

Of all the vaguely sexual metaphors Rick had made that day, this one really connected with its audience. It had been a very emotional evening for everyone, and if helping each other was the easiest way to get out of there, so be it.

Rick and Tony helped the Lockeporters form a fast-moving and orderly line at the stage exit as the fire grew faster and larger. Everyone apologized to Rick and Tony for calling for their deaths moments ago, and each apology was briskly, yet cordially accepted.

The mayor picked himself up off the floor. No politician has ever won reelection after being trampled half to death at their own event.

Knowing it was over, he used the last of his strength to climb up on stage, take out his pistol and look for Tony.

Over the years, tax purposes had made it necessary to put Tony's name as the sole stakeholder of a number of holding corporations. If the dream of Lockeport Scotia was going to die here tonight, the mayor was ready to die with it, but he certainly wasn't going to let Tony benefit financially.

"I'll be in town the rest of the weekend at least," Rick said to the last person exiting. "We'll do something, for sure. Alright, that's everybody, except for—"

He took a look back at the inferno and saw the mayor on the burning stage with his pistol pointed at Tony. Thinking fast, he pulled a rope near the stage exit, causing a heavy curtain to fall on the mayor.

"Looks like it's drapes for you!" Rick quipped.

Tony graciously pretended not to notice that Rick had said something stupid and wrong, just like any good son would for his father.

Rick and Tony ran out the door and down the alley just as the flames spread into the mayor's office and to the rum stills.

The mayor lay on his back under the heavy curtain. As the stills ignited and exploded, his final memory was of the day he refused to put in expensive flame-retardant asbestos insulation. The mayor was a retrograde man in many ways, but the decision that ultimately killed him was way ahead of its time.

39: The last crusade

Angus Junior stood at the bow of the *Bluenose* and looked at the ocean ahead. He'd done everything right this time, but the wind wasn't on his side. Just a breeze to get them out of the harbour would've been enough.

Mugsy was still catching his breath after his walk across town. All his gasping and wheezing could have maybe powered a tiny paper boat for bugs, but what good would that do?

"It's not a steep hill, but it's a gradual incline the whole way, see?" Mugsy panted. "That's what gets ya."

Gwen noticed flames and smoke behind Mugsy in the distance. She immediately began making some rough calculations. A straight line could be drawn from the gym, through the *Bluenose* to the ocean. The distance between the gym and the boat was...

She grabbed the wheel and braced for an abrupt launch.

"Okay, I'm Jakey now, phew!" Mugsy said, aiming his gun at the *Bluenose.* "Time to sink you dinks!"

Just then, East Side Mayor's blew up. All the overproof bootleg rum stills to finance Lockeport Scotia exploded at once. The resulting fireball could be seen from Lower West Pubnico. Had the Nova Scotia news media not been suffering from explosion fatigue after the Halifax one, this blast would've been just as famous.

The tremors immediately caused the rickety wharf to collapse.

"Shmaa!" Mugsy yelled, as he fell straight down into the shallow, muddy harbour.

The blast wave shot air in all directions but, most importantly, straight at the *Bluenose*. Her sails caught this sudden gale, and she launched out of the harbour toward the open sea at top speed. Gwen took the wheel and held her steady, but Angus Junior was thrown over the bow.

He landed belly first on the bowsprit and hugged it tightly, like a horizontal version of sliding down a fire pole. Water splashed his face, and the salty wind forced his eyes closed.

After a few minutes, Elias leaned over the bow. "Ang-Ju! What are you saying down there, buddy? Just shimmy yourself backwards! Take it nice and slow, I got you!"

As Angus tried to crawl backward back onto the ship, he got the sudden feeling you get when your wallet's not in your pocket. He forced his eyes open and saw the Jigtallica lyrics bottle precariously dangling by its string from the end of the bowsprit.

He reached out to grab it just as the *Bluenose* hit a wave and knocked him off balance.

"Hang on Ang-Ju!" Elias yelled. "Gwen, slow us down!"

The process to slow the boat down involved the entire crew co-operating in perfect synchronization, but as Gwen started explaining that to Elias, she realized there was no point.

Angus Junior was now dangling from the pole, holding on with both hands. His feet skimmed the water. If he lost his grip, he'd be run over by the fastest boat in the world. And yet, he reached out again to try to grab the bottle.

"Ang-Ju, give me your hand!" Elias yelled.

"But our songs!" Angus Junior yelled back. "I can reach it! Then you won't have to kick me out of the band!"

"Let it go. These songs aren't worth anything without you to play them."

Angus Junior held out his hand and Elias pulled him back onto the *Bluenose*.

The string snapped and sent the bottle into the ocean, this time for good.

Jigtallica was over. But now that Elias had accepted that human life was more valuable than a very niche musical subgenre, a real friendship could truly begin. Elias would soon hear jazz for the first time and completely forget about thrash fiddle. But his friendship with Angus Junior would last the rest of their lives.

Everyone cheered for their captain as Elias pulled him back on board. "What are your orders, Cap Ju?" he asked.

"Everybody, man your stations and listen to Gwen!" Angus Junior commanded. "Let's get the H out of here!"

Everyone cheered again and took their positions at the sails. Gwen started giving commands, and before long they were out of Lockeport Harbour. Elias took one last look back at Lockeport and saw Rick and Tony waving goodbye from the shore.

~

"Well, Tony, me b'y," Rick said, as he watched his friends sail away, "looks like we's both out of a job."

He picked up a newspaper from a pile of debris. The headline read, "Canadian Mint Announces Contest To Design New Dime."

Rick briefly considered this as he watched the *Bluenose* majestically sail into the moonlight, then flipped to the obituaries. "Hmm, let's see who's survived by who," he muttered.

"You know, Rick," Tony said, "the next mayor is going to need a lot of help rebuilding Lockeport. Or, at the very least, condensing all this debris into new piles. And...my mom isn't seeing anybody right now."

"Tony, me son, lead the way," said Rick, and they walked together toward town. "There's just one thing I still don't get...When did Mugsy go to high school?"

"He was in grade six when I was in grade eight," Tony answered. "I think Adam Knock was in his class."

"That's why I didn't recognize him right away then. Way past my time," Rick said.

He lit two cigarettes and handed one to Tony. "One of Adam's brothers was in my class, Nugget. Wonder what he's saying."

"Nugget's got a baby now, last I heard," Tony informed him.

"You don't say! With who?"

"Left field, but Amelia Mader."

"No!" Rick replied. "Wow. But I thought her and John-Gavin—"

"Oh, right, you must not have heard," Tony said. "Her and John-Gavin broke up and they are not on good terms."

"But they always seemed so happy. What's ol' John-Gavin sayin' these days, by the by?"

"Oh, he works at the new garage. Down where the hat store used to be."

"Lockeport Hat World closed?! When did that happen?" Rick said. "Start from the beginning, Tony, me son, and don't skimp on the details."

The whole walk home, Tony caught Rick up on all the Lockeport gossip.

40: Racing every way on the sea

After the explosive launch, everyone on the *Bluenose* actually worked together pretty well. They sailed as a team, and now they were in the homestretch. The fact that this motley assortment of land lubbers and throaters could sail her at all just goes to show how well designed and built the *Bluenose* really was.

The sun rose over Feltzen South as Lunenburg Harbour finally came into view. Elias had mixed feelings. He was happy to be out of Lockeport, but seeing it from so far away, somehow the town of Lunenburg seemed small.

Gwen and Angus Junior chatted together by the ship's wheel. "You think they'll cancel school today with Hennigar missing?" he asked her.

"At the very least they'll likely just have someone come in and do a piano sing along all day," Gwen answered.

Petey and Polluto lit Winifred and Florence's cigarettes.

"Yo ho ladies," Polluto said, leaning against the main mast, "now that we've got some extra shore leave, we was thinking of seeing a picture tonight."

"Boss and I heard about one where a drawing of a mouse made out of circles drives a steamboat," Petey said. "Everyone's talking about it!"

"This we gotta see!" Florence answered immediately. "That sounds like it could change the whole friggin' world."

"We gotta score some ether for that one," Winifred added.

Elias watched Rita nonchalantly file her nails. He wasn't a big fan of everything she'd done that night, but he related to her. She was the only other person on board who had nothing in Lunenburg.

Gwen interrupted his melancholy. "Sheet the sails!" she yelled. "We're coming in fast!"

Everyone manned their position and brought the *Bluenose* up to the wharf gradually and carefully. As the dock got closer and closer, Elias felt the same dread in the pit of his stomach as when he'd boarded the *Creamer* the morning before.

Old Man Feener stood on the edge of the dock with his arms crossed as the *Bluenose* glided into place.

"Hello, my ragtime gal!" Florence greeted him.

"Not funny, Flo!" Feener told her. "I could get fired for this. And you could all go to jail!"

"Only if you tell people about it," Winifred shot back. "You had fun last night, didn't you, Feen? We listened to your 90s nostalgia. Why do you wanna ruin that for everybody?"

"Tell you what, Feen," Florence told him what. "You let this one slide, Win and I will come back next time you're working and you can tell us all your opinions about Bram Stoker's *Dracula*."

This was a solid 85 years before YouTube, so the opportunity to deliver a long, rambling monologue about a 90s Gothic horror classic to an audience was rare and valuable.

"Alright, sold!" Feener agreed. "I'm going to the office to fudge my logbooks. You guys better have this thing tied up and spotless by the time Walters gets here."

Feener walked away from the *Bluenose*.

"You guys can handle the cleanup, right?" Florence asked. "We're just gonna go clock in at the Boscawen and take a nap."

"Call us later about the mouse boat!" Winifred told Petey.

The exhausted sisters stumbled off to sleep at work.

"Y'arr, we'd love to stay and help clean up, but we best get to checkin' the captain's stove. A blaze could be raging!" said Polluto. "Let me know if ye want me to take ye back to throat school, young fella."

"I will, thanks," Elias said, as he hopped off the boat.

He didn't have any real choice but to consider it. If he was going to live in Lunenburg, he would have to get by swabbing boats and cutting throats.

"Looks like we both got girlfriends now, huh, boss? That'll be a fun thing to bond over," Petey said, following Polluto down the pier. "Our anniversaries will be the same day, so we can shop for gifts together! Maybe we could even have one of those double weddings!"

Polluto and Petey started toward the captain's house, where they would eventually find that the stove was off and everything was fine. But that's a boring story for another day.

~

Gwen and Angus Junior got to work tying up the *Bluenose*. They had such an easy rhythm together, Elias didn't know how to help without feeling like a third wheel. He lit a cigarette and watched Rita struggle with her heavy suitcase.

"It must have slipped your friends' minds, darling," she told him, "but back in Lockeport, I was told my luggage would be carried for me."

Elias watched as Gwen showed Angus Junior how to tie a knot. He hadn't seen Angus Junior that focused on something since the night they wrote *Sea and Destroy*. He didn't want to interrupt.

"Where to, Miss MacMurphy?" he asked, taking Rita's suitcase.

"Just to the train station, darling. I can manage from there. Maybe a drug store along the way. You can wait outside."

Elias silently waved goodbye to Angus Junior and walked down the pier with Rita.

Angus Junior fumbled with his sheepshank. But he had so many feelings bubbling up in his heart, he couldn't focus on the rope.

"Hey, Gwen, about that gravestone thing I mentioned earlier," he stammered. "Even though we're still alive, I was still wondering if, uh, we could be boyfriend and girlfriend."

"Angus Junior, matters of the heart are notoriously difficult to forecast," she said. "I wanted to be your girlfriend today, but tonight has just been so unpredictable. I simply cannot accurately predict how I'll feel tomorrow or the day after."

"Well, uh, what would help you forecast better?"

"The only way to improve a probabilistic model is to collect more data."

"So, if we do more stuff together, would that be more data?"

"Yes. The more things we do together, the more I'd have to analyze," she said.

"What about, uh, kissing?" Angus Junior asked. "Would that create any good data?"

"I think that would produce some very valuable insights."

Gwen and Ang-Ju shared their first kiss. It really helped Gwen gather more information on kissing, to help her better predict if she'd like to do it again.

"That data was pretty convincing," she told him. "But it wouldn't hurt to collect a little more."

They kissed again. This time not for any weird math reasons, but because they liked it.

~

Captain Angus Walters Senior had taken the first train into Lunenburg that morning. He had an international championship hangover and just wanted to sleep in his own berth on his own boat.

But as he approached the *Bluenose*, his worst fear was realized. His son was messing around with it.

"Hey! Get away from there! That's a friggin' national icon you're fiddling around with!" he yelled. "It takes a man to sail a ship like the *Bluenose*, not a stammering school boy. And you're bringing a girl on there? They're not allowed on boats! Don't you know the superstition?"

Angus Junior put down his rope and walked right up to his father. "You know what, Dad? You can take that superstition and stick it in the museum, where it belongs. You may be a world champion sailor, but you're a world champion butthole, too. I didn't harm your precious *Bluenose*, so frig right off!"

As Lunenburg's most admired man, Angus Senior didn't like being talked to that way. But this was the first time he'd seen his son display any self-confidence whatsoever, so he respected it.

"Ugh, I'm going to bed," he said after staring his son down a while. "We'll talk about this later."

It was the closest thing to 'I love you' he had ever said.

He boarded the *Bluenose* and went below deck to bed.

After seeing Angus Junior stick up for her and for himself, Gwen estimated the probability that she'd like to kiss him again had jumped up a few meaningful percentage points.

Angus Junior's adrenaline was pumping harder than at any point that night. He was shaking. He needed a cigarette. "Elias, did you see that?" he shouted. "That was some Real Pipperoo stuff I just did!...Elias?"

He looked around and realized Elias wasn't there. "Gwen, I have to go. But I'll see you soon?"

A good forecaster never deals in absolutes, only probabilities. But Gwen broke her own rule. "100%," she told him.

41: Pipperooism revisited

Angus Junior ran down Montague Street, looking for Elias. He passed the spot of wet grass where he'd had his big coughing fit, only 24 hours ago. A lot had changed since then, but he needed to let Elias know that not everything had. He still needed a best friend.

He found Elias on King Street, sitting on Rita's suitcase outside a phone booth, quietly smoking a cigarette, deep in a scheme, like always.

"Oh, hey Ang-Ju, what are you sayin'?" he asked. His voice was devoid of its usual bravado.

"Not much. Mind if I skeeze one of those smokes?"

Elias got up off the suitcase and handed him one. "Some night, eh?"

"Yeah, some night. What are you saying today? I'm gonna do something with Gwen later, but I should still have time to jam tonight, if you want."

"Ang-Ju, I gotta be honest...I'm not saying much here in Lunenburg anymore," Elias said, his voice quavering. "You got Gwen and school and stuff like that. It's not fair to ask you to give that up. But thrash fiddle is all I've got."

"I love thrash fiddle too! I can do it all!" Angus answered. "We'll figure something out. We can just do less shows, maybe. Let's just have fun with it."

"I'm an all or nothing fella, Ang-Ju. If Jigtallica isn't gonna be any bigger or better than it is right now, then jamming won't be fun. All I'll see is wasted potential."

"What *are* you sayin', then? You don't wanna be my friend anymore?"

"Rita offered me a job in the city," Elias said. "Well, sorta. She says if I work as her assistant for free, she'll let me hang out in a recording studio sometimes. Maybe even let me play backup fiddle on a couple of tracks."

Back in the 1920s, doing free labour for a well-connected egomaniac was considered a good opportunity in the entertainment industry. Obviously a lot has changed since then.

"Oh, uh…" Angus Junior stammered. He wasn't sure what to make of it. He felt immense relief that he wouldn't have to go on tour this summer, but he struggled to imagine an interesting life in Lunenburg without Elias.

"Maybe you could come and stay in Hali some weekends," Elias offered. "A couple of Lunenburg boys up in the city, who knows what kind of trouble we could get into!"

Rita stormed out of the phone booth. "Are you coming or not, darling?" she asked Elias. "We simply haven't the time to dither around this historic burg any longer."

Elias looked at Angus Junior. If he saw any sign of hurt or abandonment on his face, he would've called the whole thing off. But he just saw a smile.

Angus Junior wanted a best friend, not a caged bird. He knew that Elias was a fiddler. He had to fiddle where the fiddling was good. "Have a good one, Elias," he said. "Call me when you get settled in."

"For sure. When I have time, I'll do that."

Elias would phone Angus Junior later that night, and then at least once a week for the rest of their lives.

He picked up Rita's suitcase and carried it behind her as they walked toward the train station.

"Those dreadful beasts at the radio station refuse to wire me train fare, so we'll have to figure something out, darling," she huffed.

"Hmm, Horace Heisler is working the ticket counter today, I think," Elias said. "He lost his leg to a sperm whale some years back. Got right obsessed with getting revenge on it. Anyway, last year he did and it turned out great. He turned his life around and started working at the train station."

"What frightfully tedious information, darling," she said. "If you're to be my assistant, surely you need to learn to speak when spoken to."

"I'm just saying, the man's got a soft spot for animal revenge. If you wrap your hand in some gauze and tell him we're on our way to Halifax to get vengeance on a sea lion, I bet he'd let us on for free."

Angus Junior smiled as he lit his cigarette. It comforted him to know that Elias was on to bigger and better schemes. He took a drag and barely even coughed this time.

It hadn't gone quite as he'd planned, but that day he had smoked his first cigarette, skipped class, performed on the radio, gotten his first kiss and his dad's attention. He was a fully realized Pipperoo.

They both were.

Epilogue

The year was 1981.

Three thousand, five hundred miles away from the South Shore, two California friends were having band troubles of their own on Santa Monica Beach.

"We've got the sound, we've got the skills, we've got the attitude! But let's face it, we just don't have any song ideas."

"Maybe we should let Dave back in the band."

"Quit coming at me! We're not letting Dave back in!"

"*You* quit coming at me!"

"Guys, quick! Come check this out!"

"What is it, Kirk?"

A third friend held up a bottle he'd found washed up on shore.

"Let me drink that! Whoa, wait. It's got writing inside."

"Hand that over! *Sea And Destroy*, *Master of Poopdecks*, *Saint Anchor*? What is this stuff?"

"They're lyrics, James, you idiot! And they're not bad, actually... Wait a minute. If we just change all the nautical stuff to normal stuff, there's a dozen albums worth of material in here!"

"Good thinking, Lars! Oooh, yeah-heah!"

Lars tucked the bottle into his leather jacket and they all went straight to the studio.

It was sixty years too late, and drums and guitars would be featured instead of tin flutes and fiddles, but the world was finally about to catch up with Jigtallica.

Bryn Pottie

Acknowledgements

Obviously I did most of the work on this book, but I need to shout out a few helpers! The result would've been a self indulgent ripoff of the *Simpsons* episode 'Lemon Of Troy' without notes and encouragement from a bunch of people. A useless, lemon-shaped rock of a book, as it were. Thank you to everyone below for helping me find the lemon behind that rock.

Vanessa Purdy: Our relationship changed a lot while I wrote this, but you still read every draft and gave absolutely essential and insightful feedback. You talked me out of including some real horrible ideas.

Zack Brunning, Christine Roberts, Desiree Lavoy, Sean Skerry, Kyle Johnston, and Ann and Emily Pottie each read early drafts and helped shape the final product. I can't thank you enough for your time, thoughts and encouragement.

I'd also like to thank Patricia Kobusingye for helping me pick up my flagging enthusiasm for this book after its first round of rejections.

Thank you to Andrew Wetmore of Moose House Publications for seeing the potential in this book and sanding off some rough edges.

I carefully researched Elias' misguided and ultimately failed obsession with expressing himself through an absurdly niche performing art by dedicating my 20s and 30s to sketch comedy. The friends and collaborators I met during the ups and downs of this experience shaped the writing voice I used to write this friggin' thing. Anyone I've ever taken a day off work to spend the day writing, rehearsing or taping some weird project with, thank you.

Most notably, I would like to thank Hannan Younis for *Definition of Knowledge*, Sam Rudykoff for *Newly Single Gamer*, Dylan Gott for *Fun!*, Jay Wells L'Ecuyer for *Vote Wasted*, Rob Bebenek for *Family Business*, Kenn Scott and Jeff Biederman for all their professional writing help. Donny Kehoe and Alex Maveal for *Ruth and Gehrig: Outta Left Field*, Miguel and Freddie Rivas for booking me on *Rapp Battlez!*, Sean Skerry and Brett Clarke for *Reasonable Volume*, Allison Dore for mentoring me at life and training me at two menial jobs, Ian Gordon and Phil Moorhead for countless half-finished projects that made me laugh harder than anything I've ever actually completed, and sketch troupe The Boom (Tim Dorsch, Garrett Jamieson, Dan Galea, Deb Robinson, Desiree Lavoy, Keith Pedro, Hannan Younis, Eytan Millstone, and Jay Wells L'Ecuyer) for adopting me.

Humber College Comedy: Writing and Performance Program grads of 2006—forever young!

About the author

Bryn Pottie grew up in rural Nova Scotia, then moved to Toronto to become a big hotshot writer. After bumbling around the Canadian entertainment industry for about 15 years, he moved back to the South Shore. Reconnecting with his roots taught him to truly appreciate the beautiful, magical, and inspirational place that is Nova Scotia.

The Great Lunenburglary is his first novel, and a love letter to his home.

www.ingramcontent.com/pod-product-compliance
Lightning Source LLC
Chambersburg PA
CBHW060314310726
48976CB00007B/2319